FINE D[...]

Deborah Valentine [...] London and is currently working on her fourth crime novel to feature ex-policeman Kevin Bryce. Her previous three novels are *Unorthodox Methods*, *A Collector of Photographs* (shortlisted for an Edgar Award, a Shamus Award and an Anthony Award), and *Fine Distinctions* (shortlisted for an Edgar Award). They are all published by Gollancz.

FINE DISTINCTIONS

by

Deborah Valentine

GOLLANCZ CRIME

For Michael

Gollancz Crime is an imprint of Victor Gollancz Ltd
14 Henrietta Street, London WC2E 8QJ

First published in Great Britain 1991
by Victor Gollancz Ltd

First Gollancz Crime edition 1992

Copyright © D. Valentine 1991

The right of Deborah Valentine to be identified as
author of this work has been asserted by her in
accordance with the Copyright Designs and Patents
Act 1988

A catalogue record for this book
is available from the British Library

ISBN 0-575-05337-2

Printed and bound in Great Britain
by Cox & Wyman Ltd, Reading

Prologue

He stepped out of the dark into the light without being aware of the change. The driveway was without obstruction, its surrounding walls high, topped with a snaking coil of barbed wire. The structure beyond was of a severe design, and the drive curled past it, allowing one-way entry, one-way exit, under the conspicuous eyes of video cameras. Stoop-shouldered, he trudged, hands at his sides in uneasy fists. His brief spell of euphoria was giving way to a familiar sense of doom, and it was as if he were trying to hold on to the good, keep his sense of satisfaction clutched closely to his side like the hands of untrustworthy children.

One curious fellow, alerted by those manning the cameras, came outside and stood watching his progress troubled by his peculiar stance.

Sweat met clammy, cold air and he began to shake. The pressure just below his breastbone was tight, getting tighter. He gasped. Only by some stubborn impetus of will did he manage to keep moving.

The man watching him was joined by another. This younger man was as thickset as the first and dressed in a corresponding uniform, considered young only by comparison. "Merciful hour, Dick," he said.

As he reached the main entrance, the pain penetrated. It started slowly, then shot up like mercury in hot water. He staggered, dizzy and sick. When he hit the ground, he put his hand in hot vomit and realized dimly it was his own.

1

Waving a hand, the older man sprinted lightly down the entrance steps. He had to move speedily lest Fergus, his partner, always the pushy fellow, make an effort to usurp his senior authority. "Here now, lad, what's the problem?"

Fergus tagged after, and having reached the man lying prone on the pavement, lifted his sharp nose disappointedly. "He's locked," he said. "Shitfaced."

His companion was doubtful. In any case, it was common for these men to spend their time together in the giving of opinions and counteropinions. "Looks funny, if you ask me. And he's slippery as a babe purged fresh from the womb."

"Ah, come on, Dick, smell him, if ye can over the muck. Do ye think he uses Jameson as perfume?" He gave the foot of the fallen man a shove with his own. "Ye can't be sicking up here. There's a proper place for that kind o' thing. Find yerself a bush, will ye? No point in the partaking of spirits if ye can't hold 'em down." Fergus was a teetotaler, a less forgivable folly than his know-it-all attitude.

The man on the ground rolled on his back, stared into lamplight that made the heads above him look like black spots on the sun. He blinked hard. His whole life was not passing before him as he might have expected. No, only the last hour, as if in that hour were condensed the total of his thought and experience; the highlight, the fall. He groaned.

"Look at him, grabbing his chest, he is," Dick observed, triumphantly.

"Probably hunting up another bottle under his coat—"

"Must have been in a bit of a scrape. His shoes are muddied something terrible, and look at the buttons ripped off his shirt. The back of his hands are bleeding, if you'll notice, and he's got a nasty cut on his chin."

"Probably took more than one tumble in his shameful state."

. . . had to hold on to your anger, elsewise you were nothing . . . nothing at all . . . sure, it was a true state-

ment . . . had it coming, she did . . . bloody American . . . her fault . . . had it coming . . .

"Needs a doctor" was Dick's pronouncement.

"Needs to bloody sleep it off somewhere other than here" was Fergus's.

And while the watchmen at the Berkeley Court Hotel debated his sobriety, he died.

"She was a fine-looking young woman, wasn't she? A kinder man could have chosen an uglier specimen, certainly," observed a fresh-faced member of the Garda Siochana murder squad to his superintendent.

The technicians had finished their duties, and the body was about to be removed. The two men gazed down at where it rested among the mist-soaked grass and sodden leaves. She had, indeed, been a fine-looking woman, and the strangulation had not marred her much. There was but a crust of blood about the nose, a slight red mottling of her fair complexion. With her eyes closed, she resembled a sleeping baby with a bit of heat rash on her face. But it was cold where she lay, and her body was cold to the touch. The terrible red ring around her neck indicated she would not wake up and reassure them all by crying. The superintendent sighed. They were joined by the detective sergeant, a scrappy little man of fifty.

"Never got to her knickers," he told them.

"Looks like just the thought of it killed him," said the young inspector.

"Did a bit more than think, lad."

"Oh, sure," said the lad, agreeably.

The new inspector was getting on the superintendent's nerves. Morning was never his best time, and this hour, so early, when night had not quite allowed itself to slip irrevocably into day, was particularly hard on his fragile disposition. He would have preferred to be in bed, cuddling the wife, steeling himself against the first assault on his ears of the Dublin rock and roll group his son played loudly on cassette upon arising. It was a group the super pretended to dislike but was secretly proud of, same as he was his son. He looked sadly away from the

body before him. Over the hedge he could catch a glimpse
of the walls surrounding the Berkeley Court Hotel. Finding this view as grating as the last, he turned to the
detective sergeant, who said, "It looks like the hair
threaded between the fingers of the Berkeley corpse is
probably hers. Under her fingernails we'll probably find
a piece o' him."

"Ah, well," said the super, as if it went without saying. A passing car slowed, the driver indulging his curiosity at the plethora of police vehicles. The super
glanced at his watch. Must be an American on the way
to work at the embassy nearby. Americans had peculiarly
early habits. Dublin was hardly waking yet; by the time
it did, the crew would be mostly cleared away. That was
something to be thankful for, he thought.

"She had no identification on her, did she?"

"Ah, no, sir. The lads have been searching the area
for a handbag or some such, but they've come up with
nothing yet."

"Well, no doubt she won't be too much trouble to
identify."

"She would have made an impression on the com-
munity, certainly."

"If she came from around here," said the inspector,
as if it were impossible for her to have lived in Dublin
and escaped his notice, her being such a beauty, and him
the notable lad on the prowl. The super raised his eyes
to the sky. In seconds it had lightened to the color of
stone, and like stone it would probably remain all day.

"I'm supposing it's time for us to start knocking on
doors, sir?"

"Ah, well," he said, which they all knew meant yes.
Yet they didn't move, maintaining a respectful silence
as she was covered and slowly lifted away, toward the
waiting van.

The inspector cleared his throat. "Where do you suppose he thought he was going, sir? Walking the direction
he was."

A curtain twitched in an upstairs window across the
street, catching the super's notice. Early as it was, the

neighborhood was hungry for the giving and getting of information.

"Home," the super replied absently. "That's where they've always a mind to go. Home." And with that, he walked straightaway toward the first door, thinking, as he had so often in the past, this a shitty way to start the day.

Book One

One

Events had been set into play a week before. The day had begun quietly. Kevin Bryce, having finished his breakfast, stood at the window of the house he shared with Katharine Craig and placed his dirty plate in the sink. The radio blared news of a former IRA man newly arrived back in the country. A man so indiscriminate in his violence that even the most rabid members of that group were no longer disposed in his favor. Katharine pulled the plug on the electric kettle. She was wearing a red tartan bathrobe, and her dark brown hair, which had the kind of fullness that comes from a lifetime of proper haircuts, looked particularly rich against it. Her complexion was clear enough to forgo makeup, but she rarely did and hadn't that morning. She wore just enough to accentuate the strong-boned construction of her face. If pictures were any indication, there had never been any little-girl prettiness about Katharine, even as a child. The nose was too pronounced, too crooked, the eyebrows too dark, her eyes an unsettling shade of gray. She had broad shoulders and was tall for a woman. Barrel-chested and solid, Bryce was a tad short for a man. They met at eye level.

"Let's go to Cork," Katharine said. No mere suggestion, but a subtle warning.

If Bryce read it as such, it did not show. His voice was soft, possessing a timbre as beautiful as any stage actor's, and he answered, sociably enough, "Sure. It's Thursday, isn't it? So the shops here will be closed this afternoon. I'd like to get a pheasant. One of the whole ones, complete with feathers.''

''A pheasant with feathers,'' she repeated clearly and without indulgence.

Psychologists maintain that, in the relationship between a husband and wife, a power struggle is often played out over the comparatively minor issue of driving. Who should give suggestions (turn here, park there, *Look out!*), the manner in which these small helps are proposed and accepted, the way they might be timed, are all part of the foreplay of conflict. Kevin Bryce and Katharine Craig were not married, but for the last three years, their companionship had been constant. And despite the unpromising circumstance of having come together during a murder investigation, they were, in many respects, well suited. They were both creative and solitary. They were both, to varying degrees, selfish.

Eleven years older, Bryce had been married once. At age fifteen he had fathered a son. No, not married then, he wasn't so precocious as that, but he had been held accountable for the baby, Steven. The mother had died a few months after the birth, and Bryce's parents had taken the baby in. As soon as Bryce was of age, the fiscal burden of caring for Steven had been his. Steven was an adult now, doing well on his own, but during his growing years, Bryce had carved out a career as a California deputy sheriff. It was a career he might have continued if the serious novels he coauthored with his friend James Parnismus had not actually sold and eventually sold well. He was slightly more used to restriction, so his manner of keeping his distance from people was different, if no less effective, than Katharine's.

Katharine had never lived with a man before. Working consistently, single-mindedly, at the art of sculpture, she had obtained a fair amount of positive recognition while still quite young. Collecting no cumbersome ties, moving rapidly from place to place, she had been master of her own fate, if she remembered correctly. Unfettered and self-sufficient.

Sitting on the passenger side of their Renault, Bryce put his foot on the brake. Katharine downshifted, glancing at the foot on the imaginary pedal.

"Did you say something, Katharine?"

She shook her head.

"My mistake. I could have sworn I heard you say something."

He drummed his fingers on the armrest. She gave him one shrewd glance. This was, she was sure, an oblique reference to a conversation they'd had the week before. And the week before that. And a month or so before that. It was a topic that was showing up with amazing, if one-sided, regularity.

"The fact of the matter is, Katharine, I've never met anyone less willing to talk, more *fucking perverse*, than you are" was what he'd told her.

This from a man whose books projected such a kind, uncanny understanding of human frailty. This from an articulate man, precise and accurate in his assessments. Unwilling? Perverse? Was he completely blind? She honestly *couldn't* talk. Oh, she could handle simple things like *pass the salt, please*. Or at a party she could smile, hold a cocktail, and make her observations on the weather. But beyond this, words had always seemed to her to be incendiary things, dangerous as nitroglycerin in clumsy hands. In awkward situations, she never responded verbally when a shrug or a lift of an eyebrow would do. Had learned to smile and look absently away when the question posed appeared difficult. Never apologized, or spoke an endearment, when she could simply touch. Why cloud the issue with inadequate vocabulary, bad timing, or poor delivery? Besides, she wisely concluded, your own words could always be used against you. Unwilling? Perverse? She was, to borrow one of Kevin's words (a word, by the way, he could utter with such calm diction, it had the air of an acceptable adjective), *fucking* terrified.

She ground gears. He grimaced.

"Something wrong, Kat?"

"Nothing. Nothing at all."

She put her foot on the accelerator.

A crooked two-lane road connected their village with Cork City. Twenty miles of usually wet rolling hills quilted by fences of stone or bramble. The landscape was divided into distinct colors. Dark brown where the soil had been overturned, where shrubbery, now in November stripped of summer colors, bared its basic anatomy: trunks, twigs, woody vines. Blue sky if it was sunny, as it was that day. Gray if it were cloudy. Grass provided the ever-present green. As a rule houses were white, but like any rule, there were exceptions. Cottages butted firmly and evenly one against another made a continuous stream save for one shockingly pink front. In another hamlet, a chartreuse pub stood out, a proud black sheep among the white. On the rivers, wild swans glided serenely by mud flats.

His own serenity ruffled, Bryce said: "Is this how I'm going to die? A head-on collision with a truckload of sugar beets?"

Easing back to the left, she responded tightly: "I had room."

Bryce made a low whistle.

On the edge of Cork, where the road grew wide, was a garbage dump. There white and black birds sprang up, up out of the heap at the approach of a tractor, a long, ragged line of flight. They made a graceful swoop around a group of telephone wires, light and dark as photograph negatives, then doubled back to once again delicately pursue their lunch among the rubble.

"Pretty," she said, not realizing she had done so aloud.

Bryce peered across her toward the dump, then granted her the same kindly, exasperated gaze he had reserved as a rookie cop for the wandering patients of a local nursing home.

Katharine sailed down the road without noticing.

* * *

Patrick Street is a short, congested thoroughfare through Cork City's downtown shopping district. On it, the eternal fight for a parking spot goes on, booby-trapped by jaywalkers quick and unpredictable as rabbits, double-parked delivery lorries narrowing space already at a premium, bicyclists weaving unsteadily through traffic, and taxi drivers pulling out of their designated center-lane parking, sure and unyielding. Headway is further complicated by a baffling, ill-marked series of one-way side streets jutting unexpectedly off the main.

Bryce pointed mutely.

Katharine, distracted by the blast of a horn behind her, struggled doggedly past.

"And there—"

"Where?"

"Too late." He went on, bemused. "You know, I've never been able to work out the correlation between the accelerator and the pressure you apply to it when you're looking for a parking space. Now, logically—at least to my way of thinking—it would seem sensible to apply *less* pressure, in other words, to go *slower*, in order not to inadvertently miss an opportunity to park. However, your theory appears to be precisely the opposite. Could you *explain*—"

Katharine turned sharply down an alleyway, faced on either side by cars, half on the street, half on the sidewalk. Minimal space was left for moving vehicles. She stepped on the gas. Bryce remained admirably silent for a moment before stating quietly, "This is a one-way street."

"I know."

"But you're going the wrong way!"

The car screeched to a halt. She shoved the stick into reverse, put an arm on the back of her seat and, eye on the road, moved backward with a speed that made the transmission scream. An elderly, white-haired lady crossed the alley using careful, arthritic steps. Shriveled to the point she stood hardly taller than the cars, she was a short, no-shit personality. Raising her cane, she thumped the Renault bumper smartly just as Katharine came to a stop. Bryce jumped and stared. Katharine turned left into one driveway, backed into another, set herself properly in the street, and stopped for the lady, who gave her a sour nod. Katharine then fit the car neatly into a newly vacated spot.

"Happy?" she asked, arching an eyebrow.

"Delighted," said he.

Two

Brick, brick, brick. The alley was paved with it. The buildings were built with it. Dark red and sturdy, rising three or four stories overhead, effectively blocking the sun. Yes, the shops were nice, their storefronts carefully chosen for this pedestrian byway. Boutiques, bookstalls, wine bars.

I should be pleased, she thought.

But the bricks seemed so high; and the shops so very cute.

She stopped to take a hard look at herself in a window, but there wasn't the proper light for a reflection, and all she saw were the contents on display. Platters and plates. Victorian linen. A washstand with bowl. An antiques shop. It reminded her of their cottage. Two hundred years old, its stone pristinely whitewashed, it rooms tidy-size, their ceilings low. The north windows framed an impressive view of the town harbor, of Jamesfort and Charlesfort, each seventeenth-century wreckage commanding its own bluff and, farther on, the Atlantic. They'd arrived in Ireland with two suitcases apiece and a whole lot of traveler's checks. Stumbling into the village, they'd fallen in love with the view, the convenience of a place where James could dock the boat he lived on, and a particular pub near the harbor. They found the cottage furnished and settled in quickly, despite the necessary trips for the show she was opening in London and the short jaunts they took around Ireland. Three months later, when James arrived,

15

he and Kevin started work on a collection of short stories and she began a new series of sculptures.

For her the adjustment had been fairly easy. The village was a haven for many an artist and craftsman, and she had been able to find a studio near the cottage. It was a small stone shed situated next to a pub, absolutely freezing most of the time except directly in front of the coal stove where she kept a kettle boiling constantly. The rough tables had been left by a previous occupant as had some of the tools hanging on rusty hooks. She had sent for a few of her own, keeping her needs simple, wanting to create basic sculpture using the most basic tools. And what did a writer need but pencils and typewriter and typing paper? But before settling into an upstairs room six months later Kevin had moved from room to room to room, testing every corner of the cottage, uncomfortable working in a strange atmosphere. He had been too used to the cocoon provided by his old home in California, living among things acquired mostly through his grandparent's estate.

It had been a gradual process, this accumulation of objects. Kevin would bring home an odd find from an outdoor market. Or on a drive they'd stop at an antiques shop and he'd make another small acquisition. It had surprised her, for while Kevin was not a man whom she would consider cheap exactly, he was not a man to whom the idea of waste came naturally. Too many years penny-pinching as a young deputy with responsibilities. Yet he'd bought these things, and what were they to do with them when they moved on? She wasn't necessarily objecting, just made curious.

"A writer spends a lot of time looking at his own walls," he had told her once.

That might explain (though not entirely to her satisfaction) his concern with the furnishings. What it did not explain was the amazing speed with which she had fallen into the practice. During the previous years of her adult life, her expenditures were related to essential needs. Namely: work, travel, food, and clothing. Money was rarely wasted on superfluous articles. In the back on her

mind there had always been the idea that one should stay
stripped down and ready to move. Even now, her studio
remained spartan, without distractions. But the cottage . . .

She'd been seduced in the most innocent fashion—a
day trip, a stop to stretch the legs, a shop in the process
of a stroll. And Kevin had been so interested, often
soliciting her opinion, the last thing she wanted was to
spoil his pleasure. Before too many months had passed,
she had been suggesting, all on her own, that a particular
cloisonné vase would look lovely on the mantel, or re-
marking on how nicely this crystal brandy snifter would
complete their drinks table. And the items had gotten
bigger. No longer restricted to silver-capped jars or bits
of crockery, they had moved on to tables and chairs,
armoires and sofas. Not to mention curtains and wallpaper. All found on harmless outings, all with significance. *Do you remember when we* . . . On those halcyon
days, the cottage's ordinary appointments had been
slowly replaced by purchases not easily disposed of.

Katharine pursed her lips. They had all been chosen
with a certain consistency of taste. Even now, in this
shop's window, she thought it easily possible to pick out
what would catch Kevin's eye. The crockery was un-
distinguished. The linens nice but unlikely to arouse interest. Kevin never looked at jewelry. There was an early
Battersea box; not in the best condition for a collectible,
not quirky enough to be loved. Ah, there it was. Yes,
indeed. A mantel clock. Its enameled face marked by a
discreet circle of blue and pink roses and set in a distinctly
masculine case; walnut patina lustrous and aged, lines
simple and compact. The initials G.M. had been
crudely—eccentrically, considering the elegance of the
design—carved into one corner. Was it from 1840? . . .
1820? He would make an understated comment on its
beauty and then perhaps say, *We could use something
like that*.

"That's nice, isn't it? We could use something like
that."

He'd emerged from a bookstore, brown-wrapped parcel in hand. He stood behind her and tucked it into his pocket. Katharine took a moment to ponder without conclusion the fine distinction between knowing a man, and predictability. Bryce moved away to examine the clock from another angle. No doubt he'd find the price.

"Only a hundred and twenty pounds." He seemed surprised. "Less than two hundred dollars at the current rate of exchange."

A peculiar stillness, as though she'd just been shockingly slapped, kept her from commenting instantly. They were some distance from the shop before she finally said: "You still check the rate of exchange."

"It's not necessarily a matter of checking. There are three 'bureaux de change' in the village, not to mention the post office and the banks. They all have boards posted on their doorways. You only have to look."

Katharine digested this information slowly.

"I see," she said in a tone that indicated complete blindness.

Pheasant, woodcock, and duck hung on a line tied by their crepey ankles. Produce stalls set out boxes of fruits and vegetables. Oysters in the shell were piled high. Salmon and large, flat, fresh-eyed fish were being filleted across the aisle from alarmingly dark spiced beef. In a glass case, black and white puddings were wedged between rashers of bacon. Despite the English Market's lofty Victorian ceiling and the November chill, the air was heavy and meaty-smelling. Customers moved from vendor to vendor, queued up for the local delicacy of buttered eggs.

Kevin had taken his time choosing a pheasant and was now waiting for it to be wrapped. Katharine was watching his hands. They were muscular and callused, graceful working hands. One held a stray chestnut-colored feather and was tapping the hard end against the top of the counter. It was his habit to tap things, especially when he was thinking. It seemed he could conjure pens and pencils out of the thin air for the purpose; create at the dinner table a consistent sound, steady as the drip of a faucet, with the end of a knife. The point of a feather makes no sound at all. But Katharine took Kevin's hand in hers to stop the tap-tap-tap her imagination so readily supplied.

In the labyrinth of dingy alleys of the marketplace, there was located an elegant tavern favored by fine elderly ladies for the weekly luncheon and businessmen for hearty, businesslike fare. The dining room was long and narrow, with high molded ceilings, mahogany wainscoting below gilded mirrors, and dark velvet curtains where there were no windows. The room managed to convey both austerity and warmth, as though one ought to be comfortable, though not so comfortable as to sit with anything less than the best comportment. Katharine and Bryce sat side by side in the bar, waiting with sustaining pints for their table.

"For someone who insisted on coming to Cork, you haven't done much shopping," he observed.

"True."

"Would you like to go to the movies? Or there's a pantomime at the opera house tonight."

"No."

"Didn't think so." Kevin sipped his lager. "Are you not feeling well, Kat? Did you have a bad night's sleep?"

"I'm fine."

Bryce made moisture rings on the bar with his glass. Something in this gesture's nonchalance recalled to Kathrine his interrogation of her during the murder investigation where they'd first become acquainted. It was as if with each ring he were carefully measuring out the alloted length of his patience. She was sensitive to the pleasantries, the concern for her welfare, knowing the gentle application of pressure would follow and knowing that would segue into a subtle tug-of-war. He might feel apologetic, but of course he *must* herd her in the direction he wanted her to go. She could forgive the insistence used during the investigation, but she could not tolerate him using the same method now. She dug her heels into the bar's brass footrest.

"You were very restless last night. You even talked in your sleep."

Katharine experienced the joy of spontaneous bitchiness. "Well, that must have pleased you. Did you get your quota of conversation?"

There followed a short pause in which Katharine put quite a lot of beer into her empty stomach.

"Not exactly. You mumbled."

"Poor enunciation," she responded crisply, "will ruin a good chat every time."

The maître d' was heading in their direction.

Bryce said: "When I want conversation, Katharine, I'll go to the pub. What I want from you is something entirely different."

She stood. "I'll say."

They were escorted to a table for two.

What was this rapport between Kevin and waitresses? This one was middle-aged and very stout, but young or old, pretty or a hag, within minutes he was able to establish a sort of complicity. Perhaps it was a hangover from his police days, a kind of finesse learned hanging out in doughnut shops and pizza parlors. He seemed to know the correct proportions of respect and banter, and the result was not a vulgar flirtation by any means, but a willingness to serve, to do so cheerfully. She didn't think this anything but an unconscious effort; and, of course, there was nothing wrong with it. She sighed. The beer was making her heavy-headed. Unusual. She had a good head for alcohol (an *excellent* head, James was fond of saying, wasted on someone who doesn't know how to use it properly). At the table across from them, several businessmen were lunching. A handsome member of the group met her gaze and smiled at her. She smiled back automatically.

"Kat? *Katharine?*" Bryce repeated.

"Pardon?"

The waitress was in an obviously jaunty mood. "Will you be wanting a sweet today, love?" she asked her.

"Oh. No. The cheese."

Smiling, the waitress bustled off to collect their appetizer course. Kevin began fingering a fork.

"Are you enjoying this little performance today, Katharine?"

"*Performance?*"

More than the word, more than the tone (for that was light enough), was a memory jarred. *Little performance?* Had she been asked, she would have stumbled badly over the explanations. But her emotions were finely tuned enough to recognize the belittling effect of his word choice, to catch in it the innuendo of a childish calculation she didn't feel inclined to, much less capable of. It was a bad approach to use with her. Unless he was trying to provoke her. "Are you accusing me of being temperamental now?"

But Bryce was too practiced a cop to make charges without having collected a full body of evidence. "I'm not sure that's how I'd put it," he replied slowly. "Could you supply me with a better word?"

She drowned her reply in Smithwicks, aware, without actually looking, that Bryce was handling the fork more firmly.

He said, "This is a perfectly useless way to spend the day—a waste of time, not to mention money. We can argue at home."

But the beer was loosening her tongue, unleashing a filthy temper.

"Are you putting a price on my head, Kevin? Not getting full value for money? Heaven forbid."

In the ensuing silence, the end of the fork touched the top of the table, and her eyes were on it in a second with an expression that was indeed eloquent. He put down the fork, leaned forward, and folded his hands.

"Do you love me?"

She stared at him.

"It's a simple question, Katharine. Just your type. Requires only a one-syllable answer. Yes or no."

She looked away.

"I'm just curious. In all the time we've been together,

you've never once said, I love you. That's just a little unusual.''

Her heart was beating so fast she thought she might choke. She tried unsuccessfully to swallow.

''I suppose you feel you're being articulate enough—''

''Don't tell me how I feel!'' came out louder than conversational.

Equally nonconversational, Bryce replied, ''And don't bullshit me!''

The businessmen, a table of lunching ladies, all taking a healthy interest in the entertainment provided by human drama, were putting aside their forks and soup spoons, craning their necks like curious kittens.

''Do you want to leave me?''

''Yes,'' she stated with desperate conviction.

''Well, since we've established that fact, let's establish why you want to leave.''

''Is that absolutely necessary?'' she managed to ask. ''Of course, you've had experience in these sorts of break ups before. Just like you taught me about sex, police procedure, and some of the finer points of literature, I suppose you think you have to teach me the etiquette of leaving.''

It was a perfect exit line, and she knew she should use it as such. But, like a tired traveler who had taken one step further than was wise, she felt suddenly weak. The waitress hurried down the aisle with bowls of consommé.

''That was a cheap shot.''

''Cheap shot?'' She rallied. Giving each sentence more emphasis than the last, she moved, inch by inch, further from the original question. ''You want to talk? Hear this. I don't like having my driving criticized—even when you don't say anything I can *see* you wince. I managed to drive for twelve years in a dozen different countries and do it accident-free. I don't like being picked up after. I'll throw my underwear in the laundry when I'm damned good and ready. I don't need you to do it for me. As for annoying personal habits, your tapping drives me nuts.''

(She was slowly levitating out of her seat.) "And if we're going to discuss bullshit—you don't look at the exchange rate simply because it's there; you're looking because you want to go back to the States. Well, I don't. And as for perversity, you're manipulating me through the cottage, which I hate. It's so fucking quaint, it makes me want to puke."

The consommé had arrived, and Katharine was on her feet, confronting the openmouthed waitress with the word *puke*. And Bryce was starting to laugh.

"Well, honey, you want to leave, you've got the keys to the car."

She stood stunned. Bryce studied her with one uncompromisingly cool eye. She slung her purse over her shoulder. To the clatter of china and the murmur of little old ladies, she made the march to the exit; back straight, chin level, and step firm.

Three

The sun was working hard to burn a hole in the thin morning mist but the waters of Galway Bay sparked sporadically and even then only dully. Along the Salthill promenade there were a few hardy local residents taking their exercise or standing idly as their dogs relieved their bladders against a streetlight base, their bowels on the concrete walk, preferring those inconvenient spots to the large triangle-shaped green that separated the seawalk from a modern neighborhood of large semi-detached homes. The other tip of the triangle pointed up the hill to a much older line of buildings, those providing the kind of amusements usually found at seaside resorts—the penny arcades, the quick food, the pubs and restaurants, the hotel that must have been *the* grand place for a party seventy or eighty years before. The white buildings looked grubby in the damp morning light though they still retained an appealing, if dispirited, air. It was the off-season and they had been mostly deserted for warmer climes and seemed to feel the slight, like a girl left sitting curbside after a party.

Those residents walking the promenade were bundled tight, most moving briskly. Below them on the bay's sandy shore stood a lone man, an athletic figure wearing American jeans, an Aran sweater under a navy peacoat, and a wool cap. The cuffs of his jeans were damp, his legs planted wide apart. He kept his back to the promenade. The breeze off Galway bay beat moistly against his face while he pondered the problems of a Mississippi river gambler he had read about in a book the week before. They were problems with which he could feel an identity

24

and that not only excited and scared him but also made him a little amused. He glanced at his watch then turned and, head down, sprinted awkwardly across the sand to the steps. As if taking his example from those citizens on the promenade he pulled his hat low on his forehead as he climbed, turned the collar of his coat up high.

Across the green was a house with a ten-year-old Mercedes parked in the drive. It made quite a picture, this large house with its white walls, its slate roof, the tidy front garden behind an iron gate, the car, all so much the home of a family man, all so presumptuously safe. Well, he was almost a family man himself. He stopped at a distance of about thirty feet and couldn't help but laugh. A Jack Russell puppy was running unattended across the grass, a fugitive from one of these very homes, dragging a stolen cap. The man squatted and as the puppy circled near he reached out and managed to grab the brim. He pulled, the puppy pulled. He pulled harder. Practicing future fierceness, the puppy growled.

"That's a good lad. Don't let anyone be taking your prize away. Get good and angry and give me a nip if you feel it will do you good." The terrier growled on, wagging his stump. "Oh, what a lovely little ratter you'll make, lad. Digging them out, snapping their necks easy as slicing pudding."

The door to the house opened and a man came out, tall and slim and nattily attired in a black tweed overcoat and scarf.

He watched the man come down the walk and open the gate before he stood, letting go of the cap. The puppy, having given his all, tumbled backward. Both men moved toward the car and the puppy, not realizing the game over, ran after.

It was as easy as he had anticipated. He simply dropped into the passenger seat and said, "Oh, Dennis, 'tis a fine place you've got for yourself here. Made to last, isn't it? They don't make them like that in America anymore, everything's disposable. It's an easy enough thing for the wind to come along and huff and puff and blow their houses down."

Dennis had just stuck the key in the ignition. He looked

up, too startled for recognition to immediately follow. "Pardon me?" Dennis said.

Always was the well-spoken fellow, he thought, with his cool educated voice. Pushing up his cap he allowed Dennis a more complete view of his face. Outside the puppy dropped the cap and barked. Inside the smell of Dennis' cologne was permeating the car. He judged it a good scent for a gambler to use, signifying night life and loose ladies, but a poor choice for a surgeon. Dennis' own face, as long and thin as when he had been a student, became suddenly rigid, his eyes blinking rapidly as if the glare of seeing the future hurt his eyes. Funny as the expression was it was no funnier than many he had seen, on the living or the dead. Still, it was gratifying. Dennis flinched, perhaps the thought had crossed his mind to go for the doorhandle, but in that instant he had Dennis' left wrist in his right hand and the bone of his forearm digging into Dennis' elbow, pressuring it just short of the breaking point.

He said, "Why don't we have ourselves a little jaunt in this lovely ride? Chat about old times? Oh, you were a snobbish little prig in your youth, Dennis. Do you remember?" he asked and seemed disappointed when the only reply Dennis could make was a series of short grunting gasps. Poor Dennis had gone astonishingly pale. "Will you be starting up the car soon or would you rather we went back in the house and had a cup of tea with the wife and kiddies?" Dennis' mouth was working in the most stupid fashion. To put an end to it the man released his hold; Dennis snatched his arm back protectively. Continuing softly, he said, "Why don't you start it up, Dennis. Somebody will be calling soon to be letting the family know exactly what they need to know."

Dennis sputtered the argument of any unimaginative, law-abiding citizen on a cold workday morning, "You can't do this!"

He pulled the gun out of his pocket and stuck it in Dennis' side. Extraordinarily cheerful, he said, "Would you fancy a wager on that fine point, Dennis?"

Four

Mick Cronin rose from bed at his usual hour of half noon. He made his obligatory trek to the loo, stretching his stiff back. Left. Right. Over. Up. Be careful now, it was delicate. Felt a little twinge right there, under the last rib. A few good handfuls of cold water had to be thrown in his face before he dared a look in the mirror. A slight bagginess under the eyes, a bit of puffiness along the jowls, but not too bad. No, the morning exercise would take care of that. And, in his well-considered opinion, those red veins in his cheeks added nothing more than a healthy rosy glow. Not like poor Liam. Liam's face looked like a stoplight. Mick turned sideways and went up on his toes. In his shorts and undershirt, he was still a trim figure. The mirror didn't lie. Exercise, of course. Exercise at once.

He lay on a brown paisley carpet, hooking his toes under the frayed base of a tweed sofa. One. Two. Three. Four. Puff to the left. Puff to the right. Over and under. The sounds of Dublin—the hum of cars, a siren, a jackhammer—made their assault, like the sunlight through the curtains, only penetrating so far. Stand up. Bend down. Quick—but not dangerously quick—movements. The walls, painted a dread shade of dusty orange, became but a blur. Careful again, the back, lad! The back! Run in place. Could feel a little grime from the carpet between his toes. Should give the room a sweep today.

His fifteen minutes of exertion having come mercifully to an end, Mick gave himself an invigorating rub with

27

a damp cloth, and shaved. He consumed his first meal of the day: a little tea and brown bread, some marmalade. As the reports on the radio came through, he chewed faster. The renegade called Vox had kidnapped a Galway surgeon whose name was being withheld by the police. Mick recalled having met a medical student from Galway many years before and couldn't help wondering if it was the same man. The idea produced a quick shudder. Terrible, thought Mick, buttering his bread, terrible, terrible anger.

He dressed. It was his opinion that certain indulgences were necessary, and he had fine white shirts, handmade, thirty pounds a piece, always spotless. (And should anyone comment on the expense? Well, it was his money. He'd tell that to that shagger Tommy, damn his insinuations. Right to his face.) His blue suit was clean and crisp, his oxblood tie knotted in such a way that the soup stain didn't show. Running a wet comb through his thick silver hair, he noted how very few strands came out caught in the teeth. Taking a final look in the mirror, he said, "Brilliant, young man. *Brilliant.*"

He hurried down the stairs outside his flat. At the bottom, on the banister, the post was collected. He shuffled through the piie breathlessly, hands unsteady. Maybe today. But all there was for him were a couple of bills, an expected check. He wilted a little. Still, it was sunny and crisp, leaves would be falling in St. Stephen's Green, and there was still plenty of time before Christmas.

He made his way down the street as he did every day. As though he still had an office to go to.

Liam stopped home for a midday meal. This wasn't the usual for him. Maybe it was the news that was screaming at him from every conveyance of the media. He thought the wife might need him. Might even want him to read her the reports in the *Independent.*

But she was a rock, his Nell. And if her eyes had red on the rim, well, she had the right. Finding her in their basement kitchen, he noted approvingly that she was busying herself. Two loaves of soda bread were cooling on the rack, and her special fish stew was being cooked up fresh on the stove.

"Will you be after giving me a taste, love?"

She dipped a spoon into the broth. Puckering her long, slim lips, she blew on it gently. She was a fine-boned woman, face wrinkled beyond repair. Liam could not look at her and not acknowledge his responsibility in creating a good many of those lines. He had been a rascal in his youth, not at all leery of the barroom brawl, of contact with the shady character or the one with the outlawed connections. Money was meant to be spent, drink to be drunk, and women to be appreciated for their individual charms. Sure, his mark was there, plain as if he'd carved his initials on the trunk of a sapling. Now growing older, it was territory marked deep and permanent. Her expression tugged at his heart, recalling the winsomeness that had won him so many years before, the willingness to please. She touched the spoon to his mouth.

Swallowing, he smacked his lips. "Suffers the lack of salt."

"It does indeed, and it will continue to suffer, like the rest of us." She gave a significant glance to his significant middle. "If you have a mind to kill yourself with unhealthy habits, you'll be doing it somewhere other than this house," she told him, and there was no teasing to be found in her tone.

Liam sat heavily on a kitchen chair. As he watched Nell take two more loaves of bread from the oven, his attention grew sharp. She kept her back to him.

"And I'm wondering who it is feeding you the idea that my health is in need of tending. Is it that eejit next door, Bridie Coyne?" he asked with a heat he knew a sign of trouble.

She said, "I thought you admired a woman with a rambling intelligence."

"Sure," he said, his eye on the four loaves, "but the key word is intelligence. That woman just rambles."

"It's not like you to be mean-spirited."

"And it's not like you to pay heed to her nonsense.

Can't do this, can't eat that, can't bleedin' live because it will cause your death—that is the essence of her philosophy, Nell, and you know it. Always anointing herself with oil. What does she call it?—*aromatic therapy*—like she's some Hebrew chieftain. Worse than holy water.''

"It's scientific.''

He heard the catch in her voice, but he kept on.

"It may be, but it's bloody boring the way she goes on about it. Experimenting with these mixtures as if she expects to heal the whole world with her concoctions. More likely she's going to put one wrong oil with another and nobody'll have to send a golden, prophet-chauffeured chariot for the saintly Bridie Coyne—she'll blow herself and the whole neighborhood to high heaven!''

He knew to refer to a bomb was the wrong thing to do even as it was done. She turned and he saw the tears she was trying to hide, understood the hard look even as he understood the extra loaves of bread.

"He can't come here, Nell.''

" 'Twas you who first brought him home.''

"Sure. The one regret o' my life. But there was no way of me knowing how it would turn out. That day I brought him home twenty years ago, he was just a sixteen-year-old lad on his own in Dublin. He's a killer now—one not even pretending to have a cause anymore. He kills just for the sheer joy of it.''

Nell had long before renounced Catholicism, but she could still recite her own beliefs as if they were some stubborn church liturgy.

"He's never misbehaved in this house. He's never harmed a woman.''

"Never *harmed* a woman? And what do you consider widowhood, my love? A *liberating* experience? And being left childless? Is that not harm?''

"You know what I'm saying, Liam. I'll not have my meaning twisted by your fancy talk. Besides, it may not be left up to you or to myself.''

Liam's chair ground softly into the floor as he leaned forward, his low voice strengthening its menace.

"And what is it you're trying to tell me?"

She wiped her hands on the apron she wore, and Liam didn't know whether the gesture was instinctual or symbolic. He studied her carefully.

"Has Special Branch been by to pay you a visit?"

"Oh, aye," she said, reverting to the northern vowels that had eased during her years in Dublin, "they came to poke and pry, as is their way."

A flurry of mixed emotions brought him to his feet as he asked, "It's been years since he was here last. What makes them think this time different from all the rest?"

"It seems he's paying visits to old friends. So they came, once again, to pay their respects to me," Nell said, and her wooden delivery, meant to hide the bitterness of this humiliation, did not succeed.

"I wish to God he'd stayed put that last trip to America. I don't know why he felt he had to come back."

Her eyes met his, and he saw in them the knowledge he claimed not to have. He turned his face away so she wouldn't judge the strength of his anger. "Was there anything to tell these police, Nell, when they came knocking on our door?"

She slumped, asking softly, "And what would I tell them? Would I tell them the lengths I would go to all those years ago to make sure I had your attention? Would I tell them what you encouraged because it suited your peculiar notions of freedom? How hard I tried to live up to them? Do you think that dried-up vulture of a man and that red-haired shadow of his they send to pick the bones of our memory would understand if I told them how it turned both better and worse than I could have been expecting?" Fueled by the shame beneath the surface of her resentment, she stood up next to him and made him face her. And face her he did, much as it pained him, much as it tempted his temper. "I stuck to our story. It's mostly the truth, after all, that he regarded our place as a home of sorts. At least, in the early days. And I gave them the book."

Liam stared at her. "The book?" he whispered, but felt no surprise.

"Aye. There's no secrets between us. That's been your wish from the beginning. But it came in the mails yesterday, and I hadn't the chance to be letting you know. But it came," she said, blinking rapidly, "so I gave it to them. I gave it to them because I knew you'd want me to, because I'm your wife. Even if, when you talk of criminals and police, to my mind it's a very fine distinction you'll be making. It seems to make some difference to you. Though you can't be expecting for me to turn off what became love, just because you tell me. But I gave them the book. They have it. For whatever use they may make of it." She turned abruptly back to the cooker.

His hands were shaking too badly to reach out to her. He said, "He was no Jesus, Nell, however much you may see yourself as Judas Iscariot."

But her only comment was "If he makes it as far as Dublin, it will be a miracle."

"You must believe in miracles, considering the trouble you've gone to," he said, indicating the extra loaves.

"I've been married to you for thirty years; that's a miracle in itself," she observed humorlessly. "The police want us to follow our usual routines, as they call it. But if he does make it to Dublin, you'd best stay out of the way. I wouldn't find widowhood *liberating*."

Heavy-booted footsteps cut off any reply in the making. They stood motionless, startled as always at so much sound coming from so petite a girl. Standing in the doorway wearing the paint- and chalk-smeared jeans of a student, a black jacket that marked her as a girl of unorthodox opinions, she was still palely pretty. The only possible mar on her beauty being the shaved head, in the center of which was braided the solitary remainder of her once long hair.

"What's this about being a widow and liberation?" she asked, dropping a canvas satchel down over her arm onto the floor.

"I'll probably know soon enough. Your father keeps up his unhealthy taking in of fats and salt—not to mention the liquor. I'll be a virtual bird out o' the cage, Angela."

Nell kept herself busy at the cupboard, rummaging for some spice that until that moment had not been deemed necessary. Behind her back, Angela watched her father slowly reseat himself at the table. They exchanged a look Angela wrongly interpreted as accusatory.

"It wasn't me reading her articles on health. If I were you, I'd be looking next door. Maybe after all these years, Mrs. Coyne has finally worn her down and won her ear. More's the pity for us all. If she's turned into a Coyne convert, Da, you'll be the one finding death a liberation." She flopped onto a chair.

Liam rubbed his eyes with his fingers. "After all these years, your mother has no need of Bridie Coyne. She knows where to hit me so it hurts," he remarked tiredly.

"The stomach, is it?" Angela winked at her mother.

Nell sat down across from them and folded her hands on the table as if readying herself for prayer. Her powers of recovery were remarkable, her ability to put a good face on things one of the talents that had ensured her survival as a girl in Belfast, as a wife in Dublin.

"There's a lesson to be learned here, Angela. Something you should be knowing for life with your Paul. Men always like to imagine they're abused. It makes them feel less guilty."

"Guilty for what?" she asked, more devilish than naive.

"For being what they are."

Angela wiggled her shoulders provocatively. "Lechers and bullies, every one," she said, and laughed richly.

Though she was a Dublin housewife in sensible skirt and cardigan, makeupless, her surroundings homely, Nell's smile was that of a sad and sophisticated woman of the world.

"And what have you got there in the satchel, Angela? Paints for your class?" asked Liam.

"No. Chalks this time. Paul and I are doing some drawings on the sidewalk near Trinity."

"Ah, yes, you and Paul, is it? He'll be looking out for you then. Not letting anyone give you a hard time about the way you're dressed and all." But the thought of Paul was obviously no comfort to him. And in his present state of mind, he might have made an issue of it as a diversion, or perhaps as a way of compensating for what Nell described as his peculiar notions of freedom and the muck it had made in their lives. But he was circumvented by the wise instinct of Angela, who made a sweet mockery of the notion of Paul by saying, "Oh, Da, he'll be Cuchulain himself! Felling the whole lot of them!" She made a wide sweep of the air with her hand, ending with a swoop at his forehead, where she kissed him. She blew a kiss at her mother and then she was gone.

"And *that*," concluded Nell, jerking her head toward the empty chair, "is your doing, too."

All in all, Liam decided, he would have been better off in the pub.

Five

Bryce found the bus station.

It was evening by the time he reached the village. He
took the coast walk home, the moon tagging his steps
like an old dog. The tide was out, leaving the harbor a
mud flat, shiny and damp, porous as liver and about as
fragrant. A couple of fishing boats hunkered down in the
sludge. Bryce moved reluctantly, hands in the pockets
of his tweed coat, the pheasant packed under his arm.
Somebody greeted him as they passed, and afterward
Bryce could not have said for certain who it was that
spoke.

On the outskirts of town, where the water took over
again and led out to the Atlantic, he could see their
cottage, a coy flash of white among the shrubbery. The
light in the window stopped him cold. He hadn't thought
Katharine would make it home before he did. He had
supposed he would have time to get home, to put this
bird (a ridiculous reminder of the errant rationale with
which this day had begun) into the fridge, to sit down
and compose himself before they took up round two. He
felt at a slight disadvantage that he had not been allowed
this. At the same time, it was better than he had hoped
for. She had the car; she could have gone somewhere,
anywhere, to cool off, and she had come home. Whether
it was to be an evening of reconciliation, or a grand night
of rage and turmoil, it was better than an empty house.
He tossed the pheasant into the sea, donating a feast for
any fish having a taste for bird, and started running.

A few yards from the cottage, he slowed, winded, and finger-combed the hair from his eyes. He did not completely have his breath back even as he opened the door, passed through the empty hall, the kitchen; from the conservatory he entered a sitting room where a fire of coal and peat burned brightly in anticipation of his arrival, where James had a hot whiskey waiting for him. Bryce felt disappointment smeared across his face bright as clown greasepaint.

James said, "Honeymoon over?"

"How the hell did—"

"Joe, the barman at the pub, not the grocer, told me."

Bryce took the drink and snapped: "He wasn't at the Tavern."

James sat down on a small chintz chesterfield, an antique with wonderful upholstery and terrible springs. A tall man, he sank deeply into the seat and started feeling up the sofa's arm. "No, but the aunt of the wife of the barman at the Stag's Head was." James found the button on the sofa, and the arm went down with a *bang!* He spread himself out over what was now a fainting couch and held up a gin with a twist, saying, "Welcome to Ireland. Three million people, all related, and all always more than ready for a chat."

Bryce did not find this cheering. He had gone to great pains in his life to retain his anonymity. The books he wrote with James had only James's name on them, and even one that James did not write had his name on it. (This was accomplished with James protesting all the way except to the bank.) James was the type of writer the media liked. He was extremely handsome, funny, patient no matter how stupid and personal questions, and he understood publicity. The media might also have loved Bryce, but for different reasons. He had a cop's healthy contempt for journalists, and though he understood publicity, he was not reconciled to it. They would have had a field day with him except for the fact he had outsmarted them. They didn't know he existed. In Ireland there was little media, but plenty of inquisitive fellows. While Bryce did not like it, he found it not so different from the scrutiny endured as a small-town policeman.

"Well," he said, "did anyone in this relay race know if she stopped back by the house?"

James answered slowly, with less of his natural flippancy in his manner. "Nobody has said they've seen her, but I looked in the closet and her suitcase is gone."

"So you haven't seen her either," Bryce said neutrally.

James looked into his drink and shook his head.

Bryce sighed, almost as if relieved, and said, "Well, I guess that means we don't have to wait dinner on her." He sipped his whiskey. "Are you hungry? I'm starved. My lunch got interrupted."

They took a walk through town to a wine bar where over the past two years the chief cook and sole owner had learned to cook a steak rare. Salad, chips, steak, and red wine were consumed in the company of revolving guests. The owner's wife and very pretty daughter were the first to join them. (The daughter sat very near to James, a man who always treated the ladies with consideration.) The owner came and went, according to the inclinations of his business, at times bringing to the table various friends and acquaintances. If Bryce was not exactly jolly—was he ever?—he at least encouraged everyone to drink, which was near enough the same thing. And he was always a good listener.

It was late when they started for home. Though this was a small village its fine harbor had been attracting foreigners since the year 1000. Vikings, Normans, Spanish, English. Now heads of foreign corporations intrigued by the possibility of developing Irish industry would settle here briefly, attracted by the village's location near Cork city and airport, only to eventually leave as discouraged as they had once been intrigued. Artists and writers, both foreign and domestic, were drawn to the beauty of the locale, or to its history, or perhaps just to the proliferation of pubs. Seamen from the grainary boats made their regular stops. Sportsmen came to sail or fish. The mysterious expatriate, looking for El Dorado or run-

ning from some private hell, comfortably monied or living hand to mouth, settled here believing they had found
what they were seeking, some for a time and some for
the rest of their lives. The locals took it all in stride,
seemingly happy for the profit and the entertainment
value these comings and goings provided. And Bryce
had been pleased to feel that he was not part of a trend
to "find" an unspoiled beauty and contribute to its ruin
but was merely part of the village's continuing flux. A
small village, yes, but a lively cosmopolitan one. The
pubs, just closing, sent revelers out to migrate noisily to
the wine bars, the only places they could legally get a
drink past eleven o'clock. Young women giggled together before disappearing inside for a last Irish coffee;
in the cold, men stood on street corners saluting their
comrades. The storefronts hadn't changed much from the
eighteenth century; the houses displayed a sampling of
Georgian doorways as fine as any Dublin had to offer.
Except for the electric lights, the Super-Value grocery,
the occasional sight of a parked car, it seemed time had
been arrested. Dogs could be heard fighting in the black
distance. High heels echoed on cobblestone curbs like
horses' hooves.

Under Bryce's leadership, they were heading down
the quay to the harbor docks, where James lived on a
thirty-three-foot Hans Christian cutter, alone except for
the sporadic visits of an attractive young woman from
London and the more regular attentions of the harbor
cats. With the onset of November, there had been talk
of him moving into town, talk of him moving in with
Katharine and Bryce, even talk of his moving to London
into a flat he kept. There always was this time of year.
James talked but didn't move. After a gale-force night,
they sometimes came downstairs to find his wet Wellies
in the hall outside the spare bedroom. But this was rare,
and Kevin suspected his taking refuge there had less to
do with the weather than with a certain state of mind.
James had been a friend to Katharine since she was a
girl, a partner to Bryce for many years, had been their
link before they became lovers. There was a solidarity

of feeling there, the sense of family. Bryce stole a sideways glance at him. Tonight, on Bryce's part, there was the irritating knowledge that James's history with Katharine went back further than his own. They had never been lovers, but James had been on the sidelines of her life, watching her pecularities nourished by the tragic events of her family, knowing things she was unlikely to tell. Right at that moment, James was balancing himself on the edge of the quay. It measured a six-foot drop from the stone dam to the water below.

Bryce said, "I'm not sure you're sober enough to pull off that trick."

"I'm almost sober. Certainly sober enough to walk." James paused thoughtfully. "Perhaps not quite sober. enough to mind my own business."

"Let's get you home quickly then."

"Don't be so cool, Kevin, that you make an ass out of yourself."

"I'm not the one who left."

"No, you're the one who let her keep the keys to the car. Did you pack her lunch while you were at it? Tell the waitress to package the soup to go?"

They arrived at the docks. On the boat ramp, a swan stood on one leg, head tucked under a wing. The metallic clank of rope against mast rang out like church bells.

James finished with "You didn't think you were going to *change* her, did you?"

Bryce took a snifter of brandy with him to a room he found chillingly tidy. It had been his own advice to himself to go up to the bedroom, try to divine her intentions from what she'd taken, from the state of the room. Tried-and-true procedures could confine pain, keep anger within boundaries. Besides, he didn't know what else to do. He'd gotten everyone in reach as drunk as they would allow, certainly drunk enough to confide, but had received no information. Nobody had spoken to her, nobody had seen her leave.

And what was he to deduce from this unnatural order? Though there was no hint of it in her appearance, Ka-

tharine was a slob. She never hung anything in a closet
when she could drape it over a chair, never put away
shoes when she could create an obstacle course of them,
rarely closed a bureau without leaving tufts of fabric
exposed between the drawers. On her bedstand there was
usually a half-finished mug of cocoa or a sticky snifter
of Grand Marnier. This, of all times, he expected the
room to be a disaster. But under the quilt and feather
duvet, the bed was made, the pillows plumped. Rugs
had been straightened; oak chairs, once draped with
clothing, stood stripped. The bibelots on her bedstand—
the atomizer, the stones and shells collected from the
seashore, the enameled box where she kept her few pieces
of jewelry—had been neatly arranged and—Jesus
Christ!—*dusted*, he realized as he lifted the lid of the
box. Her jewelry was gone. So was the travel clock
usually kept on the stand.

The armoire door, always cracked open, was securely
shut. The dresser drawers uniformly closed. He opened
the armoire first. He had to look hard to figure out what
was missing. A leather skirt, a flannel skirt, a silk blouse.
A couple of pairs of jeans were probably gone, though
he couldn't tell for sure. At the bureau he saw right away
a favorite turtleneck had been taken, and there was
enough empty space to accommodate two pullover sweaters. He might have found so few items removed reassuring if he hadn't known she could live for weeks with
this combination. She was the first woman he had ever
met who knew how to pack light. He opened another
drawer. Most of her underwear was gone.

He sat down heavily on a fat chaise scaled for a child.
He'd bought it because Katharine loved it. She liked
eccentricity, he'd learned quickly enough. Her brand of
it was stamped all over the house. The snifter he drank
from was a perfect example of the logic involved. He
wasn't sure he liked the way it looked. It had a lot of
cuts and was very heavy. But she said, ''It's not so much
how it looks but how it feels in the hand.'' And it did
feel good, substantial. This sensuality governed her
choice in everything she brought into the house. ''Never

let good taste spoil your sense of whimsy'' had been her provocative teasing when he'd hesitated over a watercolor of an ambiguous beast in Victorian dress. It was the way something made you feel, no matter how flawed, irregardless of taste or antiquity, that was important.

Bryce took a deep sniff of brandy. *"You've been manipulating me through the cottage—"*

Of course he had. He'd only meant to buy a few things, trying to establish contact so he wouldn't feel so much a stranger in a strange land. But when she started showing an interest, he encouraged her. For one, it made him feel good to buy things that gave her pleasure. And on neutral ground, it was surprising just how much you could get her to say, how her enthusiasms could reveal her reasoning. Before long, he recognized how truly advantageous these little pleasures might be. Bryce knew the value of history in a relationship, knew something about the nesting instinct, knew also how many women used a home as an extention of themselves, became houseproud, attached. That Katharine might be susceptible to this had seemed unlikely. She had her work to define herself, but it appeared she could make the house itself an art form. And unlike her sculpture or his writing, it spoke of them together. It wasn't the things per se but the memories attached that became something binding.

Something binding.

Jesus.

He tapped a finger against the snifter, watched flesh hit crystal, send waves through the liquor as if in slow motion. He didn't actually see this, his imagination supplied the details, trying to crowd out the humiliation that came when it was painfully evident your little mannerisms were getting on your partner's nerves. And yet he'd laughed.

Of course he'd laughed. He wanted to be the voice of sanity in an insane argument. He wasn't being unreasonable. He wasn't asking her to intellectualize her feelings, to list her reasons for the attachment, to shout her emotions from a mountaintop, or even confide them to their circle of acquaintances at the pub. Just to me. *To me!* he thought with all the vehemence of a gorilla beating his fists against his chest.

You've had a real influence on the direction of her work—

Had he? Could the blatant sexuality of her more recent pieces really be credited to his account? That was saying too much. Her last show had been made up of only bits of bodies. Fingers in a head of hair, the head an empty cavern, the fingers pulling too harshly for casual contact. She made use of the suggestively poised finger, the slim, exaggeratedly long hand in the small of a thick back, the masculine knee pressed into the soft underside of a feminine one. Each work concentrated on a solitary point of touch and while the bodily part might be sometimes ambiguous the intent was not. It was true that when she needed a male anatomy she used his. But what of the implied brutality that marked some of these pieces? The hand wedged ridiculously between tightly closed thighs, the teeth pressed so deeply into a shoulder that live flesh would be left torn, the escalating roughness in the texture of the last pieces that was not crude technique but rivulets in the material suggesting the limbs themselves were withering. She could put a hand against a cheek and make the onlooker see a slap as easily as a caress. If he was partly responsible for the tender eroticism of this work did it not follow he might also have influenced its cruelty? He didn't believe it.

Did you think you could change her?

Yes, goddammit, he did.

After all the companionship, the affection, the experiences they'd shared, she was still covering her ass. And, dammit, he was tired of tiptoeing around her. He got up and shoved the rugs into a heap with his foot. He had never known a woman who wouldn't say, I love you, even if she didn't mean it. He knocked the pillows to one side, pulled the covers off the bed. She thought she could evade the issue by putting her arms around him. (Generally, she could.) He made a simple request for information, and what he got was the revelation of the cartoon character who has walked out on air. Yessir, he had just witnessed decision making at its finest.

One stroke of his arm sliced the doodads off the bed-stand. Money and children, the practical dependencies that glued a couple together in the worst of times, didn't exist for them. And the only way for him to measure the effect of his presence on her emotional life was this methodical walkout. If left him to conclude that, as for companionship, a dog could have done as well as he had done. Shit, she could have all the companionship she wanted; all she'd have to do was sit in a pub by herself for an hour. Opening the armoire door wide, he yanked her clothes from the hangers. Oh, the sex had been good, sure. But he wasn't so vain as to think she couldn't find another lover who was just as satisfying.

Turning to the bureau, he opened the top drawer and tossed the remaining underclothes into the air like confetti. It made him feel stupid to think he had been so easy, to think that he had been a convenience. He dumped the sweater drawer onto the floor. He had a right to know how she felt. He had the right to be needed. Was he expected to not have feelings? To be strong and silent? An *island*?

He chucked the snifter through the window. In the terrible silence following the crash, he was surprised to note the room looked almost normal.

Six

Mick focused on the top of the stairs.
Made an effort to tread on the steps as lightly as the danc-
ers he saw dancing on the pub's telly. Arty farty airy fair-
ies, every one of them, he was sure. But, by God,
wouldn't it be something to be able to spirit his body up
to his flat the way those young lads could, making no
sound at all. Didn't look so difficult. Up on his toes, he
attempted one of the moves. His body spread upwards
over a half dozen steps with an echoing crash; his chin
came down smartly on the landing. He blinked. Lying
very still, he waited. He could see a light coming on and
hear the voice of his father's replacement for Mick's dead
mother saying, "Jim-*my*!" Then the murmur of voices
floated by, the sharp crack of a slap, and a wail.

"She's a strong, healthy girl. She can give as good
as she gets." So said one of the neighbor ladies. One or
two of the others nodded their heads knowingly. A sweet
was shoved into his mouth and the flavor of peppermint
was overpowering.

Mick turned his head slowly. There was no light at
the bottom of this stairwell. No curious peeking from
behind cracked doorways, no high-pitched inquiries into
what was only his business. Mouth dry from whiskey,
there was no one to sniff and complain of his breath. He
got up and climbed the rest of the way to his flat with
steps that sounded heavy as disappointment.

This was Liam's fault, of course. He never drank so
much when Liam was there, there being more conversation to break up the flow, so to speak. But tonight
there'd been no Liam. No bloody message. No bloody

nothing. Sure it was a bit out of Liam's way to meet in
a pub in Ballsbridge, but not that far. Practically on his
way home. Certainly not as far out of the way as it was
for Mick. Could go around the corner, serve him just as
well. Ah, true. Maybe not. There was a lot to be said
for Ballsbridge. Sure. There were people downtown with
some dreadful long memories, whose speculation was
more damning than the truth. After all, he'd really done
nothing, had he? Nothing much. And you never knew
who might be walking in, either. Especially now. With
him back in the country, on the loose. Wouldn't want
anyone thinking he was keeping up that connection. No,
it was over and done and hadn't been much in the first
place. Best to stay in untroubled territory. Nice being
close to the American embassy. Sure, it was. The best.

In his flat he left off the light, using instead the col-
lective radiance of the street. Through the thin curtains
it was possible to share the glow of lamps that were not
his, of cars he did not drive, of businesses he did not
work for, like they were all one big family.

He got into bed. Between sheets cold as ice water, he
thought of his Maire.

Liam lay in bed with his eyes closed. He was trying
hard, but sleep refused to come. He had not followed
his "usual routine" this evening but had stayed with
Nell, and they had a row that spanned the last thirty
years. It might have been going on still if not for the
return of Angela with her Paul, and then Liam had been
subjected to the slow torture of watching them together.
He would have almost preferred to argue, but Nell never
did like to argue in front of the children, preferring to
keep their miseries private. Later, outside on the landing,
he'd overheard Nell tell their daughter, "Your father's
the best man I ever met, though that may not be saying
much." It was said in an encouraging tone, though what
it was meant to encourage, Liam didn't know. Certainly
not himself.

Now in her sleep, Nell was holding on tight. So tight
that if she hadn't been such a frail woman and he such
a mound of flesh, she might have crushed him.

* * *

In a small southwestern Ballyanywhere, a Special Branch policeman held a machine gun and pressed his back against a freezing stone wall. He eased toward a window. Cold as it was, the window was cracked open. Heavy curtains obstructed the view inside, but he could hear the squeak of an iron bed. At his signal, the rest of the squad made ready to move. Professionals, yet there wasn't one of them who didn't have a wet moon highlighting his armpits, who didn't feel the potential for death coax his finger closer to the gun trigger. Too many others had died, too many times he'd slipped away, making fools where he hadn't left bodies. Like a desperado out of the cheap western novels he reputedly admired, the man known as Vox had vowed never to be taken alive. No one could afford to doubt his sincerity.

The small square of stone cottages had been evacuated. Lights and tellys functioned, preserving a thin illusion of activity. In a chess game of positions, each man on this special team played his part, moved quietly toward the door or covered the window with the point of a rifle. A street or two over, someone whistled "Dixie," and the tune carried unusually well across the night. A sergeant raised a loudspeaker, prepared to give his ultimatum.

The man nearest the window suddenly raised his hand. Inside, there started a low rumble that built and built, grew higher and higher, until it reached a pitch that touched the superstitious nerve, recalled the banshee's wail. It was the scream every man felt in his gut, if one he might never express with so much abandon.

The squad stayed stunned for a moment, even as the sound diminished. The window squeaked. Someone trained a spotlight on the widening gap. No one noticed the face in the window. They saw the bloody smears on the glass and knew who it was.

The man nearest the door kicked it in and began firing. But the cottage was empty except for the handless surgeon hanging from the window.

Ah, well.

Book Two

One

"This rain must have been sent from Waterford. Look what I found in the grass." James set a brandy snifter on the kitchen table.

Bryce hardly lifted his head from his lunch. At the casual glance, the snifter seemed undamaged by its fall. The rim was still solid, but he saw some of the diamond points on the bowl had been chipped. Before him was a plate of eggs scrambled with sweet sautéed onion, and fresh tomatoes, pâté, and brown bread. He resumed eating.

James sat across from him and poured a cup of tea from the pot. "Breezy in the bedroom these days, Kevin?"

"Not too bad. There's a board over the window."

"Yes. So I noticed. Hence my walk in the garden. Curiousity finally got the better of me."

Bryce finished the last of his eggs and pushed the plate away. James peered down at it, chose pâté and tomato from among the leftovers, put them on a slice of bread, and ate. "The food here is more consistently edible since Katharine doesn't take her turn cooking."

Coming from anyone else, this observation might have been crass. James stated it as though his interest was academic and the improvement subject to doubt. To Bryce's ears, it carried a faintly reproachful ring.

"I don't suppose you've heard from her?"

Bryce had to work hard to get out a civil "No."

James looked away, rubbing his nose, a small gesture

which irritated Bryce beyond belief. But it was when James cleared his throat Bryce felt moved to say, rather forcefully, "What are you afraid of? That she's going to die from eating only her own meals?"

Startled, James took the question literally. "She's probably gone back to eating in restaurants," he said.

Gone back. Sounded like such a simplistic solution. Just *go back* to whatever you were before, just snap your fingers and be done with it. *Gone back* had close ties to the accusatory phrase *sent her back.* (But to what? Nothing horrible. She'd done fine without him before.) *Gone back* had a final ring to it: a door closed, a segment of life completed. He was aware he was pulling words out of context. He knew he was being unreasonable.

"For Chrissake, James." Bryce got up and put his plate in the sink. From the window he could see two men at the seawall, fishing and smoking.

James touched his hands to his chest. "I apologize, Kevin. I woke up breathing this morning. My mistake. It's just that she's been gone for days now without contacting either one of us. Maybe something's happened."

Bryce opened the window and took a deep breath. The air smelled of the rain to come and cigarettes.

"Something did happen. She woke up one morning, thought, 'My God, what have I done?' and then she undid it." He closed the window.

"Don't you think you ought to make some inquiries?"

"No." Bryce turned. And some part of him that always remained detached, observant, found an angry James an interesting phenomenon. Like Halley's Comet, it was a rare event, cause for study and conjecture. Because James was easy going, because his speech sounded a little too well educated, because he was so very handsome, because he drank more than he ought, all this excess led to the general assumption James was weak. But once angry, he became neither childish nor petulant nor easily confused. Perhaps his greatest weakness lay in the fact he was so seldom angry.

"I don't think Katharine's herself right now."

"And who do you think she might be?" Bryce inquired politely.

The force of James's fist on the table rattled his cup and saucer.

"*Goddammit*, Kevin. This is a peculiar country and she's been locked up in this village for so long—"

His intensity came as a shock first, a revelation second, then a surprisingly pleasant surprise. Bryce knew the well-placed word had an excellent chance of sending James's fist in his face. And he had to admit, be it a primitive solution to frustration and inadequacy, he wanted to beat the shit out of something. That James was taller, heavier, and seven years younger made Bryce aware that more than wanting to hit, he wanted to *be* hit.

"She's not locked up now, James. You want to play finders keepers, go right ahead."

The face of that all-American boy hardened into a sharp and unfriendly strength. He secured his hands in his pockets. After a moment he rose slowly from his seat and moved as far away from Bryce as kitchen space would allow. From across this pitiful distance, he was able to convey his perceptions with a dignity that made the back of Bryce's throat tighten.

"You manipulative son-of-a-bitch," James said quietly.

Shame was not an emotion to which Bryce succumbed easily; the silence went on far too long. He kept his eyes trained on the table even as James moved in his direction.

"I think it's time I made my exit while I can still do it gracefully. I'll leave you to do something really useful, like—" James took the snifter and set it determinedly in Bryce's field of vision "—chuck more of the crystal out the window."

A minute later, Bryce heard the door slam. But as if to demonstrate how easily bad habits formed, he did not run after James to make amends before the breach could widen unpardonably. Could not battle this stubborn lethargy of spirit, knowing how effortlessly a request for forgiveness could segue into a maudlin plea for sympathy. Well, if he could not do what was right, he would proceed with what was practical. He reached for the snifter. Disobedient muscles fumbled it, and it cascaded foolishly from hand to hand to the floor, where it busted outright. Squatting, he retrieved the largest piece, the stem connected to a shard from the globe. Bryce rubbed his face with the back of his hand and it came away damp.

There was a heavy knock at the door. Bryce tossed the stem back with the other fragments and scrambled quickly to his feet. Hold on. He turned on the faucet, put his face in a handful of cold water. I was a bastard, I know. Another knock and, taking a dish towel with him, he dried his face as he went. He yanked open the door.

"Ah, Mr. Bryce, Mr. Kevin Bryce now, is it?"

The question was rhetorical, spoken by a man of about Bryce's own height, perhaps ten years his senior. His face was one easy to visualize on a cadaver, the skin being but a thin crust for the skull beneath. He was accompanied by a beefy man in his late twenties, whose red hair and bright freckles provided one hell of a contrast with his blue suit. Bryce could not recall having met either of them before.

"Mr. Bryce, my name is McGarrity. Special Branch. This is Inspector Dunne."

Of course. He knew they were police. Seeing the attitude from the reverse angle had stalled him for a moment. It was the messenger with bad news.

"Yes. Hello," he said.

"It's an eighty-one Renault you own, isn't it? A little sedan. Haven't sold it off now, have you?"

"No."

"Ah, well, sir, I've some bad news for you then. Perhaps we might trouble you to invite us in so we could have a little chat in comfort?"

Bryce had rarely heard an order so charmingly issued. He hooked the towel around the back of his neck and escorted them into the sitting room. It occurred to him that this must be a very unusual sort of bad news, for there was a key ingredient missing in their approach. The gentle hush of sympathy. Motioning for them to take a seat on the disguised fainting couch, Bryce chose for himself a stout straight-backed chair, one with enough cushion to keep him propped up, enough arm to give him something to hold on to. McGarrity cast an eye over the couch and took the match to Bryce's chair. Dunne, perhaps less schooled than McGarrity in the disadvantages of fine old furnishings, sat with reckless abandon and was rewarded by a long drop onto a hard stud hidden under the upholstery. He then surveyed their respective positions ruefully.

Bryce also surveyed their seating arrangements and found in them additional support for his feelings. Their triangle was such that to speak to one would force him to turn his profile to the other. While one studied his face, his partner could observe his hands, draw his own conclusions from the nervous fidget of the legs, or whatever body part the officer deemed most revealing. They were positioned for interrogation. Each could take his turn, shifting him from side to side.

McGarrity's blue eyes were large, filling the whole of the gaunt socket. He considered Bryce, giving him the opportunity to speak first. Bryce didn't.

"If you'll pardon me for saying so, you're not looking too well," said McGarrity.

"I don't feel well," Bryce deadpanned. He kept the towel around his neck, a hand clutching each end.

"Ah, no, no wonder, no wonder." McGarrity fished in his pockets and came up with a pipe and a pouch. He started packing tobacco into the bowl. "Mr. Bryce. It is my understanding that you have lived in this house for some two years with a lady companion, a *Miss* Katharine Craig. Is that so?"

"Yes," he replied, but he was not unwise to the subtle communiqué contained in the question. Everyone in the village had assumed that they were married. Neither one had bothered to disillusion them. Katharine, because she never thought it her duty to correct the misinformed; and Bryce, because he had come to enjoy the assumption to an embarrassing degree.

"Craig is a northern name, as I recall. Would Miss Craig have a bit of Irish ancestry in her background?"

"I wouldn't know."

"Wouldn't you? That's funny. Americans, in my experience, can be so peculiar about ancestry."

Bryce didn't respond.

"Ah, well, anyways, last Thursday week she left during a midday meal at the Tavern in Cork City. Had something of a disagreement, had you?"

"Something of one," Bryce said quietly.

"Took off in the little sedan, did she?" McGarrity set a match to the pipe and puffed.

"She did."

"Have you talked with the lady since?"

"No."

"No?" McGarrity's expression encompassed both inquiry and disbelief. "Are you sure?"

"Positive."

"That leaves me with something of a puzzling situation, Mr. Bryce."

"I thought you said you had bad news."

"My puzzling situation is your bad news." In McGarrity's strict reply, it was possible to discern the flint in his attitude. The beefy Inspector Dunne sat, as much as the sofa would allow, with a certain readiness, as if on signal. "It strikes me as funny that you wouldn't be after demanding information about the lady, seeing how we've been sitting here." McGarrity puffed steadily on his pipe.

Bryce made sure his movements were slow, kept his hands where they could be seen, latched firmly on the ends of the towel. He leaned forward, keeping his voice low and steady as he imagined the pleasures of sticking that pipe up McGarrity's ass. He said, "I used to be a cop, but I'm sure you know that. It's obvious you've run some kind of check. In *my* experience, this isn't the approach taken for the conventional bad news." Bryce stopped to look from one man to the other. "Let's put it this way. If Katharine is in a hospital or a morgue, while we've been sitting here playing patty cake, I'm going to break your fucking neck.''

McGarrity's teeth clicked thoughtfully against the pipe mouthpiece. Bryce kept the corner of his eye on Dunne.

"Fair enough," concluded McGarrity. He sat back and crossed his legs, but the tension in his partner suggested McGarrity was far from bending. Bryce wondered how McGarrity would signal his trained animal to relax. Throw him a biscuit? "Your Renault was found abandoned in a field a ways outside of Limerick. In the opinion of the experts, it was found in such a condition that the only fit place for it would be the junkyard, sorry to say. The area was thoroughly searched, and no likely driver was to be found.

"Now, there's lots of bloody young twits that would love to nick a car like that. Joyridin' is a real problem, especially in Dublin—"

"But the car wasn't found near Dublin," Bryce interrupted sharply. He knew in hoping for a linear progression, he was sure to be disappointed. This was Ireland, after all.

"To be sure, it wasn't. And neither has the car been reported stolen." McGarrity paused reflectively. "We were talking earlier about the question of ancestry, Mr. Bryce."

Bryce stared.

"As I was saying, Americans can be so peculiar about ancestry. So romantic. They come here looking for the little people under the gorse—" two of McGarrity's fingers walked across the air, illustrating the search "—or so I fancy. Hard to tell what they expect to find, exactly. Dunne here, on several occasions, has been told he has a nice Irish face—not by anyone he's been interrogatin', mind you, but by American tourists. Now, what sort of face were they after expecting him to have? Palestinian?''

Dunne had a pugnacious face, one that might topple into belligerence at any handy provocation. Bryce could see that his nose had, long ago, been broken at least twice. And set casually. It did not look like it had been broken in a very long time. Bryce wisely refrained from commenting. He asked, hoarsely, "What did you find in the car?"

But McGarrity was in no hurry to get to the point.

"Ancestry, Mr. Bryce, that was the topic of discussion."

"Katharine does not support the Provisional IRA, if that's what you're hinting. We did not come to Ireland to 'look for the little people'—" Bryce mimicked the accent well "—or to be surrounded by nice Irish faces, whatever they may be. We came for peace, privacy, and the chance to get better acquainted away from the influence of some bad memories."

"The IRA had been resurrected from sure death by Irish-American funds and enthusiasm more than once."

"Not by ours. Katharine's enthusiasms are limited, and I am notoriously tightfisted."

"That's what your captain said, too. Your being tight-fisted, I mean."

McGarrity talking to his ex-captain gave Bryce pause.

"His exact words were 'cheap little fucker, until he thinks no one's looking.'" McGarrity interlocked his fingers and stretched, cracking his knuckles. He looked like a man with all the time in the world. "Have you heard of the man popularly called Vox? Used to be called Vox Populi—voice of the people—until the people decided they didn't much like what he was saying, much less what he was doing."

"He's the object of the manhunt. But the Provos disassociated themselves from him years ago. He's a freelance thug."

McGarrity rotated the pipe from one side of his mouth to the other. Dunne began studying a hangnail, frowning painfully.

"True enough. Used to kill for a cause; now he kills for lack of a better occupation. Extortion is his favored means of support. When he's in your country, he can go about his business hardly creating a stir. Another criminal, more or less, makes no difference in America. But when he's in this country . . . well, it's very small, so he makes a sensation. Have you been following his case in the papers?''

"The last I paid any attention, he'd kidnapped a Galway surgeon," Bryce said, but felt suddenly disassociated, reserving a part of himself: the part that would hold together the outside while the inside fractured like the crystal on the kitchen floor.

"Ah, yes, well. The surgeon was taken at gunpoint outside his home in Salthill, just as he was getting into his car. He then drove Vox to a town in County Clare. It was in this town we found the surgeon three days ago, and not a minute too soon for his life, though a bit late to save his practice. He'll not be doing surgery anymore. Vox cut off his hands.''

Playing straight man to McGarrity's little joke, Bryce asked, *"Why?"*

"The car broke down.''

Two

Dunne had been dispensed to the kitchen to make tea. Outside, a darker set of clouds had rolled in. Day took on the close confinement of night. Through the sitting room window, a hill could be seen in the middle distance. On it a lone tree cast a silhouette against the dull sky, bare branches suppliantly upraised. The surrounding grass was garishly green as an old movie that had been colorized. Bryce bowed his head.

McGarrity was standing by the drinks table, where he had picked up a leather-framed photo. James had taken the picture outside the DeYoung Museum in San Francisco, a day or two before Bryce and Katharine had left for Ireland. Borrowing a camera from an accommodating (or uncomprehending) Asian tourist, James had snapped them laughing at the skillful antics of a one-legged gull. Bryce was kneeling in the foreground; Katharine kneeled behind, her arms around his shoulders, their heads together. Caught unaware, they turned out an excellent photo. McGarrity surveyed the picture at length then he replaced it slowly, apparently troubled, or perhaps it was just that he had observed in that supremely carefree couple something worthy of his disapproval.

Dunne, having made himself at home in the kitchen, came in bearing a tray of tea things and set them on a footstool. The making of tea was one of his specialties, a function he could perform when his other talents were not required. He handled the teapot daintily, filling each cup to the halfway point. McGarrity took a bottle from the drinks tray and topped them with Bryce's whiskey.

Cup in hand, McGarrity settled back in his chair, saying, "We found three sets of prints in the car. One of them yours. Another set unidentified, but I think we can safely assume they're Miss Craig's. The third belongs to Vox." McGarrity read Bryce's puzzlement with reasonable accuracy. "You'll be wondering at his carelessness in so simple a matter as fingerprints. His behavior so far has been a wonder to us all. You've heard he's vowed never to be taken alive?"

"I assumed that was bravado in the face of limited choice," Bryce said.

McGarrity grunted, took a sip from his cup, then changed the direction of his narrative. "He started off the lad with a cause. Fine-looking boy with a personality that pleased. But there's some dreadful hatred hiding in the most cheerful fellows, and so it was with Vox. It didn't really show at first, his hatred, how plentiful it was. No, it seemed it was directed at the Troubles. Not surprising. He came from County Antrim, after all. Lost one or two members of his family to the Troubles and another lot in an accident with a lorry. Wound up somehow on his own in Dublin, where we suspect he reinforced connections made in the North. He rose quickly in the ranks. He chose a certain mode of expression—violence—and made himself an expert. He was brutal, ruthless, and quick. He might be described as a kind of dark perfectionist. Those who knew him early on say he had a mean sense of humor."

Bryce's lip curled. "Like cutting off a surgeon's hands."

"Bit of a throwback to his Provo days, that seemed to me. He knew that surgeon in Dublin many years ago, although not in his illegal activities. Anyway, jobs are a big issue in the North, the idea of a man's livelihood being cut off. Putting it this way, if he'd picked an Orange dancer for retribution in those days, he'd have cut off his legs. He has the gift of clarity."

They were quiet while Bryce absorbed the implications of his special brand of clarity and humor.

"He preached a doctrine of anger. There was dignity in anger, to turn the other cheek was to leave it open to destruction, to lose one's anger was to lose one's balls. To be sure," said McGarrity, "that's not necessarily wrong."

Conscious that his sympathies were still being tested, Bryce did not openly agree. "And he had no balance to all this? No adopted family? No love?"

There was a twitch at the corner of McGarrity's mouth, the beginning of a smile swiftly lost. "Something to make him wish for peace, you'll be thinking? Ah, sure, he was a lonely sort of fellow, for all the company he kept.

"There's a lot who regard the situation in the North as hopeless. Maybe there was a point where the goal became the next hit, not ultimate peace. What would ultimate peace bring a man like Vox anyways? Revenge was what he wanted. It takes a fearful lot of energy to keep up his level of anger. Most men don't have it. More and more of his time had to be spent with his own kind. By his standards, even most of them were second-rate in their anger. I often wonder what the infighting, the betrayals, the general incompetence of the IRA, must have done to his mind, such as it was."

McGarrity sipped away the remaining portion in his cup appreciatively. "Of course, it's my opinion that peace never mattered to him in the first place. He wanted to beat the shit out of what he thought were his enemies, and when he found that not satisfyin' enough, he took on the whole world. Liked the feel of his pocket lined with other people's cash. It's surely a powerful sensation, to have a man beg for his life down on his knees before you, like you were God himself. Criminals are all alike, aren't they? Terrible conceited or just plain stupid. Most of the time both. Vox isn't stupid, he's something worse. You see, I've come to believe his vow never to be taken alive is more than a bit of bravado. I believe it's his intention."

"Are you saying he wants to die?" Bryce asked tightly.

"In Ireland you've no likelihood of being revered unless you're dead," McGarrity said, matter-of-factly.

"Do you think he will be revered?"

McGarrity shrugged. "Why not? The world has a history of it. Look at Robin Hood. Or even your Billy the Kid or Jesse James. Nasty little pricks, every one. But the world builds legends around them because they give the establishment the bird. Isn't that what most people would like to do? It's easy to mold the dead into an inspiration; the real thing's no longer there to contradict you with his perversion. I tell you we'd all be better off if Vox had simply taken up rock and roll—then it'd only be our ears he assaulted." McGarrity started lighting another bowl.

"You're saying you think he may be deliberately setting himself up for legend status." Bryce was finding this difficult to accept.

"What I'm saying," McGarrity told him, puffing impatiently, "is that he chose a certain way to live, and it's by that means he shall die. He thinks it's poetry, the poor fecking eejit."

Bryce sank back in his seat and practically whispered, "So he'll go spectacularly, taking as many of your men as he can, all in the interest of his little show."

McGarrity and Dunne exchanged a look Bryce didn't see. He had tilted his head back, closed his eyes to relieve the sting in them. Dunne got up and went to the drinks table. He poured a whiskey neat and touched Bryce on the shoulder. It was a medical touch; competent, meant to be comforting.

"*Sirrr,*" he suggested gently, "have a wet."

Bryce had ignored his spiked tea, but he took this and swallowed rather than risk being rude. Satisfied, Dunne returned to his seat. It crossed Bryce's mind that Dunne was probably good with children; could envision him pressing sweets and biscuits on a legion of ragamuffins, using a strong arm and a soft tenor voice.

Bryce asked McGarrity, "Do you think he has someplace in mind for this gunfight at the O.K. Corral?"

McGarrity snorted, half-amused, half-aggravated at

the reference. A grin marked Dunne, transforming him for the briefest second into an appealing gap-toothed kid with too red hair.

McGarrity said, "There's a man and his wife in Dublin that we keep an eye on when Vox is acting up. As far as I can tell, they've never been involved in any of his illegal activities, but he lived with them off and on for the first couple of years he was in Dublin. The man took pity on him, bringing him home from the pub one night, and it was a connection that took. We know the man tried to get him on at Guinness, where he was employed, but Vox would have none of it. Didn't want to wind up some poor old tosser at a brewery. The world was to know him, so quotes anyone who made his acquaintance then. O' course, those poor people had no way o' knowing just how he was to make his name. I've kept an interest in these people because, though he hasn't visited them in many a year, anyone who knew him in the early days will testify that he had an affection for them. Took an interest in their family rituals. It seems the wife can't read. It was their habit every evening to sit down together, and the husband would read aloud to her and to their children. When Vox stayed there, he was read to as well. Sounds very cozy, doesn't it? He's never made a connection quite the same, so it wouldn't surprise me if to this day he regards this place as a home of sorts."

"Under what kind of circumstances did he leave them?"

"Friendly or unfriendly, you mean? Difficult to say. But my guess is, since he hasn't been back for a visit— not in twenty years—the leave-taking was less friendly than they are willing to admit. Have ye read Montague's *Death of a Chieftain*?"

"Yes," Bryce said, "I've read it a couple of times since I came to Ireland."

"Well, the book was a favorite of the wife's, one they came back to time and again. The title story became something of the same for Vox. His interest in the Americas dates from this time. Started a fascination with cowboys, Indians, bank robbers, the whole nonsense.

Anyways, when he left their home the last time, the wife gave him their copy as a gift.'' McGarrity reached into the pocket of his coat and brought out a book worn so its binding was comprised chiefly of tape and rubber bands. He set it on the tea tray. "Last week the wife received it back in the post.''

Bryce picked it up and leafed through it reluctantly. "Seems he can even pervert good taste in literature,'' he said. "And what was the wife's explanation for him returning the book?''

"How did she put it, Dunne?''

Dunne cleared his throat. "She said, maybe he doesn't think he's going to need it anymore.''

"Odd story for him to take as a favorite. The saga of a mad Ulster Protestant.''

"Confirms my belief the IRA was nothing but an excuse for his natural inclinations.''

"Do you think he knows you monitor these people?''

"Whether he does or he doesn't, this is a signal to us something's afoot,'' McGarrity said.

"Yes.'' Bryce paused. "He sent it to the wife, not to the two of them? What is your impression of the lady?''

"She's a woman with no liking for the garda, I can tell you that. At one point she became quite the hostile one with me.''

"When was that?''

"Vox was very fond of her. Did a lot of talking, the wife and him, while the husband was off at the brewery or the pub. I asked her if she never tried to use her influence to discourage him from the path he was taking. Bristled right away, she did. Told me, 'Either he's a man and I don't have to tell him or—' Now what was the next part, Dunne?''

Referring to Dunne was an affectation, a technique developed by McGarrity to make himself appear less threatening than he was. Bryce wasn't fooled by their cute interplay.

"'Or they're like most men, still looking for a suck on their mammy's tit, and then it's no use,''' Dunne repeated, coloring as though grieved deeply by the allegation.

"The vulgarity surprised me. She's usually so well-spoken, a very polite woman, trim, nicely dressed, perhaps forty-five. She didn't seem the sort," McGarrity said, wagging his head prudishly.

Bryce was surprised she hadn't snatched him bald-headed. "Is there something the husband and wife are leaving out of this story?"

McGarrity needed no broad hint to his meaning. His eyes regarded Bryce steadily, underlining his seriousness. He said, "They're an old married couple; their secrets are their own. I take no prurient interest in other people's affairs."

Bryce did not feel it his place to argue. In this case, McGarrity was probably right anyway. "So you believe he's on his way to Dublin?"

"I think it's possible, after reading the story. The chieftain is on his way to expire in the dark pool. *Dubhlinn*. Eejit." Disgust twisted McGarrity's face into a mean caricature of itself. Taking the pipe from his mouth, McGarrity stabbed the air with its stem. "What I want to know is, what is Vox doing with your woman? I can see how he got the car, could be stolen certainly—but then, why hasn't it been reported stolen? I'll tell you something, we've no precedent for this. Our investigations show he's had ladies for his pleasure, but he's never been rough with them in his criminal activities, never taken one hostage, never done one any damage."

"Never done one any damage?" Bryce repeated harshly. "How many children does the average family have in Ireland? For that matter, it's not just an Irish issue. If you take away a woman's husband, in many cases, aren't you taking away her livelihood? Perhaps her place in society?"

McGarrity stuck the pipe back in his mouth and sucked on it noisily. He looked at Bryce like a hunter confronted with some as yet unspecified breed of game. Finally he said, "Never thought of Vox as the type to initiate equal rights for women. But sure, could be interpreted that

way." Slowly he added, "Jesus, you've a nasty turn o'
mind."

Bryce stared at the final drop of whiskey in his glass.

"Your woman's an artist, isn't she? A Californian.
An independent sort, living with a man without the sanc-
tions of God or anyone else. Would she have picked up
a man in a pub, do you think?"

Bryce didn't know if he was being confronted with
crude prejudice or a test of his willpower. He approached
it like a cop having to make known the indisputable facts.

"As a child, Katharine was taught not to talk to
strangers. As an adult, she carries that advice too far,"
he said, but could not keep a trace of irony from coloring
his delivery. "It's unlikely she would have picked up a
man in a pub."

McGarrity turned down the corners of his mouth in
thought.

"Can't see him hitching, he's too recognizable," said
McGarrity. "I have another question for you. Do you
happen to know the type of your woman's blood?"

Bryce felt the question was rushing up to him through
a long, dark tunnel, confusing the words.

"Pardon?"

"The type of your woman's blood, do you know it?"

Bryce's no was a purely mechanical function of his
mouth.

"Ah, well, that's too bad. Found blood on the car seat
and on the carpet. Nobody's bleeding to death, mind
you," McGarrity said as if this news might conceivably
prove reassuring, "but he surely wasn't feeling too well.
The type of the blood was O. If you were after knowing
your woman's type, we could eliminate the possibility
of it being hers."

But if this casual bringing up of the blood was staged
specifically to jog Bryce's perceptions, it failed.

"No, I don't know her blood type," he whispered,
"and I can't see any circumstances under which she
would willingly accompany your man. You know a lot
about him," he observed rather more loudly.

"Sure, we even know the color of his arse-hairs.

Everything but where he is now and what the bloody hell
he's doing with your woman," McGarrity said, irritable
as a wife deciphering the behavior of an errant husband.
"It isn't like him."

"Ireland being the way it is, I'm surprised he's gotten
as far as he has without anyone knowing," Bryce said,
suspecting McGarrity of having more information in reserve.

"Oh, there's plenty of people that knows—but we're
not among them. He's gotten this far because in Ireland
we've perfected the art of—what do my American cousins call it?—*peer pressure*." In McGarrity's smile could
be seen both sweet satisfaction and the cruelty of a man
who did not waste his mercy on the undeserving. "But
it's a device that can be used both ways, as you are
aware, Mr. Bryce. We've a fair idea where he's going,
and it's a sure thing we'll know soon where he is."
McGarrity got up and knocked the tobacco ashes from
his pipe into the fireplace. "You said you came to Ireland
for—what was it, Dunne?"

"Peace and privacy, sir, and the chance—"

"Yes, privacy," McGarrity said, with his back still
to Bryce. "Ireland being such as it is, a very small
country with time on its hands and God's overdose o'
curiosity, it seems a funny place to come for privacy."

"As a cop, I got used to small-town scrutiny."

McGarrity turned to him. "Was she? Because I'll tell
you something. That's no culchie you've got on your
hands, lad," he said, jerking his head toward the photograph.

Bryce drank the last of his whiskey.

"No," Bryce said, "she's no culchie."

"I'm told you write under another man's name."

"Yes."

"Do you like being a writer more than you liked being
an officer of the law?"

"I'm not sure there's that much difference in the
jobs," he said, and McGarrity shot him a look that made
Bryce feel oddly duty-bound to explain. "First of all,
they're both exciting jobs. But as a Tahoe deputy, I'd

sometimes sit in a car for hours surrounded by snow, waiting for something to happen. As a novelist, I've done the same thing before a sheet of paper in a typewriter. Both have a risk-taking factor. In writing, there's less physical risk than emotional, you have to be willing to examine yourself very carefully, but either one can produce that rush of adrenaline that lets you know you're alive. You risk public criticism in both fields. You're also subject to the feeling that people outside the business won't understand what you're doing or why you're doing it or the kind of humor you have to develop to distance yourself from the whole mess. You have to be interested in human nature, be a psychologist if you don't mind the word, and look at situations from all angles, suspiciously. People, in turn, are suspicious of you. What are you going to write as opposed to who are you going to arrest? I've done undercover work and sometimes found the roles difficult to shed. In creating characters for the page, I've done exactly the same thing.''

McGarrity took his place across from Bryce and sat on the edge of his seat. His voice was low and tough, and spit formed at the corners of his mouth.

''You talk of risk, of public criticism, yet you don't put your name on your work. So there's a bit of bullshit in your character, lad. You've a liking for subterfuge and self-protection. You've got the guts to take this risk you speak of, but at the same time, you try to keep what's important to you close to your heart. Is that what you're doing now? Are you tired of these emotional risks and longing for a physical one? You can't be playing a lone hand with this situation. If you know something, if you've had a ransom note or some such thing, you'd best let us know. You can trust us to do our best for your woman.'' McGarrity searched his face. All Bryce could offer him was the sight of a man defeated by his lack of knowledge.

''I do like being a writer better than I liked being a cop. The police business is behind me now. And even if it wasn't, this is one situation where I'd want all the help I could get.'' McGarrity began to look a little defeated himself. Bryce laughed softly. "When we first came here, we met a poet, and soon after, the poet and I started playing chess every Monday night at the pub. It wasn't long before he found out I'd once been a cop. He told me I must learn to stay on the civilized side of town."

"And have you been able to find it?" McGarrity inquired.

Bryce smiled sadly. "Since I've been with Katharine, I've met artists and writers whose work is sensitive and graceful, well-educated and supposedly intelligent cronies, who can only be classified as outstandingly rude to my middle-class American upbringing. As a cop, I met dope dealers and rapists with, if not better, at least comparable natures."

"Comes as no surprise to me," said McGarrity decisively. "And your woman, what does she have to say about these fellows?" Still fishing, McGarrity would make the most of any opening.

"Fuck 'em. She's able to say it very cheerfully."

McGarrity let out a frustrated gust of air. "There's no logic to this. A woman who, according to the local lads, is quiet, sticks close to her man, a good woman, may now be traipsing around the country with Vox."

Sticks close to her man, a good woman. Bryce resented the narrowness of the equation even as he wished it were true.

"I think your suicide idea is bullshit," Bryce said.

"If he wanted to live, he'd have stayed in America," responded McGarrity rather mildly, perhaps regarding this argument as one of the many forms of denial with which he was forced to cope in his profession. "Look at the surgeon. Almost shot him ourselves, we did. Surgeon passed out when he got the ax. Woke up just as our lads showed up, saw the damage, and screamed bloody murder. Scared the shit out of us. Then, having done his bit to take ten years off our lives, he goes into shock. When we were finally able to question him, he knew exactly where Vox was going, to some wayward associates in Limerick. Could have drawn us a map. O' course, by the time we got there, he was gone, leaving a bit o' damage behind him. Good riddance on that account. We're going to get him, Mr. Bryce, but I'd rather catch up with him on a country lane than someplace like Merrion Square or Two College Green, if you'll be perceiving my logic.''

Bryce did and made his request urgently.

"Let me work with you. If you've talked to my old captain, you know my reputation is good.''

"Sure, it's good. That's why we've been treating you with such gentleness. Consideration of a former officer in good standing.'' McGarrity rubbed the back of his neck and gave his careful consideration to a spot on the ceiling. "You know, there's rumors about you in the village. Rumors you're not so 'ex' as an instrument of justice as you claim to be. This being the village it is, full of blow-ins—artists and foreigners and other such riffraff—the rumor is that you're the head of the CIA in Ireland. You've heard this before?''

Bryce had. The rumor had previously been the source of much amusement between Katharine and James. Bryce wasn't entirely sure James hadn't started the rumor himself.

"Before me, the money was on a local spy novelist, and before him, a retired American security systems analyst.''

McGarrity looked at him. "Sure and they're not out of the running yet. But you're the current favorite.''

"You have to know that's not true. You know who I am.''

"Ah, sure, I know. You're an ex-cop who writes books without his name on 'em.'' McGarrity chuckled unexpectedly. "The day of your little disagreement, one o' the local lads saw her heading toward Bantry. If you be out and about and someone should ask you what you're up to, and if they're curious enough to make a call to Dublin Castle, there'd be no one there to contradict any rumors that might arise. After all,'' said McGarrity, "gossip is not our business, is it? Now, one last question. Where's your loo?''

* * *

Dunne was putting the tea things in the sink. Bryce took the crystal the tidy Dunne had earlier swept into the dustpan and tipped it into the garbage.

"Mr. Bryce," Dunne said, pulling a card from his inside pocket, "here's our number at Dublin Castle. He didn't mean to be unfriendly to you as a fellow officer, but some Americans wouldn't know the difference, you know. They'd still see Vox as a 'freedom fighter.' McGarrity had to be sure."

"Would he be sure, from just that questioning?"

"He says supporters aren't subtle about it. He says even if they lie, you can see it in their eyes, the color o' their skin, and even their smell. To be sure, it's not a popular smell with McGarrity. Vox or the IRA. That's why he had his pipe out in your house without asking your pardon. Has very fine manners usually."

Bryce looked puzzled.

"Didn't know if you might be the violent sort."

Bryce remained bewildered.

"He's good with his pipe. Put out more than an eye or two in his time." Dunned squinted his own eyes, troubled. "An' he uses 'em all—the pipes, I mean. Every one, no matter their history. I always feel it a bit in me stomach when he smokes."

Dunne sat in the driver's seat of the car. McGarrity got in beside him.

"Do you think we'll find her alive?" Dunne asked.

"Feeling a bit optimistic today, are you, lad?" McGarrity turned his head, steamed the window with a sigh.

"Do you think it's possible she isn't with him at all?"

McGarrity turned down the corners of his mouth and wagged his head back and forth.

"Well, if she isn't, then our Mr. Bryce will find her. And if he knows more than he's admitting, we'll soon know. Lit a fire under him, we did," McGarrity said, and put a match to his pipe.

Three

Bryce ran a finger down the cat's back. Insulted, she jumped off the coil of rope and strolled crab-wise down the docks toward the yacht club. There she habitually took her afternoon tea of fish guts. Bryce reread the note posted on the boat hatch. In the intervening seconds since he had read it last, it had not altered into a more agreeable message.

Went to London. James.

He looked at his watch. Amends having gone the way of a bus to Cork Airport, like any man of sense, Bryce ran to his usual pub.

"Kevin, come on now, I haven't much change left to spare." Joe the barman was a handsome lad of thirty-five; never married and never likely to be. He had a West Cork brogue, considerably toned down so the tourists could understand him, and an air of discretion bred from having lived most his life in a town of fewer than sixteen hundred, where one did one's best to keep one's custom, especially in winter, when there were fewer tourists to rely on. He was alone with Bryce in the bar. Bryce was standing at a pay phone using some remarkably bad language, none of it directed at Joe.

The pub occupied the downstairs portion of a two-story structure that had been, many years before, a house. Small windows broke up the front facing the harbor. Stone walls kept it chill enough that a fire was lighted, even in summer. The furniture provided was the most comfortable kind of Victorian. The bar was all wood: very small, very polished, very pretty. There was no beer on tap, a strike against it in this beer-conscious society. But the company was usually good, a tight circle of locals and blow-ins, some friends, some feuders, and the chess games superb. Bryce had heard it said this place was more like an English pub than an Irish one. He was not enough a connoisseur of pubs to be sure of the difference. He was, however, knowledgeable about phones. Phones were the mainstay of any cop. He knew this phone to be a phenomenally lousy one. Before the last coin had fully dropped, he was already cut off, and he cursed this fact. He cursed the fact he had no phone of his own. He cursed the fact that in this country, there was a two-year waiting list for a private phone. And he cursed the fact that they had never applied for one, as if that simple act might have implied more commitment to the country, and to each other, than they were willing to admit. He cursed it all. Most of this cursing continued aloud.

Joe came around the bar and took the receiver from Bryce's hand.

"You're doing yourself no good, nor me either. If you want to go on having James paged at the airport, use my own phone upstairs, will you? We can work out the money matters later."

In James's spare missive, Bryce had read a disturbing determination. But even as upset as James was, he didn't think James would have ignored the page. It might have been news.

"Thanks, Joe, but he must be in the air by now."

Perhaps it was just as well. "I told you so" would hang between them bright as neon. Joe hung the phone up and took his place behind the bar while Bryce stood thinking.

"When's the next bus leave?"

Joe was looking out the window. Across the harbor stood the village's only modern building, an ugly Erector Set–style hotel, and next to it, a petrol station from which the bus was just lumbering away. "There it goes," he said. Bryce saw what Joe saw and, knowing the bus impossible to catch, began a new round of filthy language that left Joe openly amazed. "Lovely. Grand turn o' phrase," he remarked admiringly.

"And I suppose that's the last bus for the day?" Bryce asked.

"Ah, sure it 'tis." Bryce was staring at a brandy snifter left by a previous customer. After an anxious glance at his window, Joe set it quickly behind the counter. "There's one coming back, but none going out. And what would your plan be now?" he asked. Bryce was heading for the door.

"To use my thumb."

Joe looked pained. "It's going to be a nasty night."

Bryce stopped at the door to say, "Yes." The clouds were already pissing rain.

Caught in a sense of urgency he did not completely understand, Joe said, "Let's take the Cadillac."

The Cadillac was a Fiat. The paint was oxidized, the body dented and scraped, the bumpers fastened by wire. It ran with coughs and sputters and ominous screeching sounds, bumping its way through the rain and coming night with surprising speed. Surprising not only because of the car's condition, but because of the way Joe drove. Joe did not drive easily, for nothing came instinctively. He kept his eyes on the road and clutched the wheel, each motion a decision of life or death. His driving affected Bryce like fingernails scratched across a blackboard. And any speed he drove was too slow.

"I don't mean to be prying," Joe said, "but I heard you had what looked like the garda by your place today. Is that why we're going to Cork? And would you be telling me where we're going once we get there?"

"I need a car, Joe, and there aren't any rental agencies in the village. I have to try to retrace Katharine's steps since she . . . left. Our car has been found, but without her in it. Special Branch thinks it might have been stolen, but they don't know for sure since it hasn't been reported missing."

Joe repeated the words "Special Branch" under his

breath. After a few moments of watching the windshield
wipers shove rain uselessly from side to side, he said
suddenly, ''I've always thought she was a lovely woman,
you know.''

The announcement struck Bryce as odd. He had not
solicited Joe's opinion, and sensitive to the use of the
word *was*, Bryce could not help but feel the sentence
flavored by an inclination to speak well of the dead.
Unsure of what sort of reply he expected, Bryce glanced
at Joe and felt his heart stop. Joe was taking a nervous
hand from the wheel and making the sign of the cross.
Bryce cast a fearful eye on the road to face whatever
disaster Joe saw in the oncoming traffic. *Fucking Irishman.* Bryce ground his teeth. They'd only passed a roadside shrine. To keep off the tender topic of Joe's driving,
he asked him, ''Joe, do you know Vox? Or do you have
a cousin, or a friend, or a friend of a friend, who might
have connections with him?''

For all the surprise Joe showed, Bryce might have
been questioning him about the weather. He said, ''Are
ye asking me in your official capacity or in your unofficial
one?''

Bryce wondered if being in the CIA would make a
difference in Joe's attitude or if this was just an example
of God's own overdose o' curiosity. He made his reply
a careful blend of honesty and tact.

''I'm asking because I'd like Katharine back in one
piece, if it's at all possible.''

Joe nodded appreciatively. ''He came into the pub
once, years ago. Had quite the winning ways, especially
with the ladies. Spent the evening dancing and drinking
and singing and reciting poetry he claimed was his own.
Found out later he'd kneecapped a man in Limerick that
afternoon. Seemed to have cheered him to no end. But
he has no strong ties to this particular area. He's not
somebody I know, nor would I ever care to. Not the best
thing for a healthy state o' mind.''

''There's a rumor he's on a kind of suicide run,'' Bryce
said.

In the glow from a passing headlight, he saw Joe scowl.

"Why? Because he can do as he likes in this country. Are they saying he's being flamboyant, showing off, because he's wanting to die? They must have gotten themselves a fancy publicity man with a flair for the romantic. He's doing what he's doing because he can get away with it, because they're so incompetent, he can flaunt his wicked ways. I'm telling you, Kevin, I never saw a man who loved his own life so much. The taking of other men's blood makes him strong, like some fucking vampire, gives him the rush o' life. He'll do his business and leave the country. Probably catch a plane right out o' bloody Shannon. He came in, didn't he? He can go out. Comes and goes as he pleases, seems to us. Him wanting to die is unlikely. Maybe he just thinks he's invincible. Or maybe the garda are thinking exactly what he wants 'em to think. The poor bastards need all the help they can get if they expect to put an end to the likes of him." Joe clutched the wheel with greater determination. "Even if you don't find her in one piece, you'll keep her, won't you? Her absence has not exactly brought about an improvement on your disposition."

"Are you telling me I'm a son of a bitch, too?"

"Too?" Joe was either too discreet or too preoccupied to press his curiosity in the matter. "I wouldn't go so far as to say that. But you know, she doesn't have much small talk, and she's always going to look as if she's got the world at her feet. People misunderstand that. Maybe even yourself, sometimes."

Bryce had lost his girlfriend, and alienated his best friend and colleague; he could hardly afford to batter his favorite publican and only means of transport to Cork. What kept him from doing so was not the basic conviction that Joe was right, but the appreciation that Joe had taken the time to try to understand her, that he was an intelligent man, an impartial jury.

"Maybe," Bryce said.

"She comes into the pub sometimes for a whiskey or a cup of soup in the afternoon when it gets deadly cold in that shed of hers. I tell you sometimes I don't know how she stands it—very hardy she is for an American. You can tell how her morning's been. If it's been good she'll be excited and even chat you up a bit. One day she comes in and says to me, 'Joe, I did brilliant work today, Kevin will be so impressed when he sees it.' 'Well, o'course he will,' I tell her. And, you know who was in here and overheard her? Old Tammy, sitting on the windowseat with his boxer bitch. Remember how the bugger got before he passed on? Pissing and moaning all the time, couldn't see though he could hear well enough, and kept getting one lad mixed up with another? Aggravated him to no end, the infirmities of old age. So he says, loud enough for the whole pub to hear—'And why would you be want to impress him? Who is he anyways?' Well, she gets up and sits next to him, taking his hand. 'Tammy,' she says, real proud of you and full o' herself, 'he could be anything. A poet, a scholar, or the head of the friggin' CIA.' Then she bought him a pint. Pleased him no end. I thought she was having him on about the—you know.''

Apprehension pinched Joe like too tight shoes. "She is the love o' your life, isn't she? And not just another member o' the CIA, for that would surely be a disappointment.''

"What if I told you she was not a member of the CIA at all?''

Joe appeared to consider this seriously. He said, "Prefer to come to my own conclusions. I fancy the idea, even if it isn't so. Didn't sit well with me, her taking off like she did. This way, too, well, I can't see Vox having much appreciation for her company. He's Irish, after all. We enjoy looking at American women the same way we enjoy looking at the things in the National Museum. Nice to see, but the upkeep would be a bit wearing on a fellow. I like imagining that she's had some training in taking care of herself against someone like him.''

Bryce would have liked to believe that himself.

"Do you think she was bored, Joe?''

"With Ireland? She surely had to be,'' he said, speak-

ing with a young man's prejudice. Bryce hadn't meant
Ireland.

"It was her idea to come here, you know."

Joe was thoughtful. "Yes, well," he answered finally,
"maybe she was in love and didn't know what she was
saying."

Bryce started laughing. Joe hadn't meant to be hu-
morous, didn't know what it was that Bryce thought
funny even as Joe started chuckling with him. He only
knew the silliness helped relieve the tension in his gut,
that it was convulsive, uncontrollable, and good. Before
they'd gone another quarter mile, they were gasping for
air like a pair of schoolboys giggling over a dirty joke.

In Cork, Joe pulled into the bus station. He told Bryce,
"It's getting late. Even if we take the time to find the
rental agencies, they'll be closed by now. There's one
last bus to the village tonight. You take the Cadillac. It
doesn't look good, but it will take you anywhere you
have a mind to go."

Bryce didn't argue. He slid into the driver's seat as
Joe got out. Joe held the door open, letting the rain pour
in. He wanted to say something. Say he knew Bryce
would find her, that she was safe and sound and in reasonable temper. But he ran into the same brick wall Bryce
did. If she was safe and sound, why hadn't she reported
the car missing?

Joe waved a hand feebly and closed the door.

McGarrity sat back away from the fire as if he didn't
need it. He did need it. It was cold. But for a man his
age it was a sad thing to acknowledge that he never had
the knack of making a proper fire. So he did not acknowledge it, he pretended the fire was of no conse-
quence or, better yet, a job beneath him. Dunne was an
excellent firemaker. Dunne had a domestic side that
would rival any woman's. Perhaps it was all those years
growing up, being the caretaker of his irritable mum that
had trained him. McGarrity didn't know. Maybe some
men were just born having the knack for comfort. It was
a valuable asset in a second-in-command, especially for

McGarrity who had neither wife nor children nor the desire to acquire any. When Dunne was cold, he built a fire. Dunne's inward thermometer was sensitive. On the rare occasion it failed all McGarrity had to do was say, "There now lad, don't stand there shivering and annoying the hell out of me!" and Dunne would build up the fire. It was a complicated ruse for a trivial problem but a good case in point. In his line of work he had uncovered many a complicated ruse for many a trivial problem.

McGarrity poured himself a whiskey to combat the cold and picked up a report from the pile of paperwork before him. It contained his notes from the Kevin Bryce questioning, a complication he could have done without. He did not want any dead Americans turning up, or French or German or Japanese or anyone that smacked of tourism or could potentially generate the interest of the foreign press. His was a small country, but he loved it. This was no abstract devotion, this was passion. Every man was an ambassador for his country and if ever a country needed a worthy ambassador it was Ireland, if ever a country deserved one it was Ireland. She was a country that sincerely needed its tourist dollars since there was so little industry. She was a country that, in his opinion, suffered much from sensationalism in foreign press accounts, ones that did not bother to separate fact from a rollicking tale, who did not bother to balance the bad with the good.

McGarrity was irked by Ireland's violent reputation when he knew so many of its citizens lived peaceably— the North included—concerned for their families and whatever bit of prosperity they could come by. A big country could take its blows in stride, but Ireland could so easily be done serious harm, was so easily violated. Nobody *had* to come to Ireland for anything but recreation and, if they had the inclination, genealogy—and why should they come if she were dangerous? He wanted to present her clean and shining and beautiful as she was meant to be. He wanted to keep Vox a private family problem, not an international one. Kevin Bryce seemed a reasonable fellow, an intelligent one, but a fool could see he cared too much for that woman. If she turned up dead, as it was likely that she would do, would he suffer silently? A man who had power with a pen, would he not wield it? McGarrity was uneasy. Kevin Bryce had his own country and McGarrity wished he had stayed in it.

The door opened suddenly. Dunne had returned from his assignment. The room was long and he walked its length waiting till he was face to face, one knee to the floor, before he said anything, as if that would impress on McGarrity how seriously he trusted his information.

"That phone call I think is the real thing, sir. There is a fellow called Sammy Bean, he is wanted in America, and he does have a boat. According to the local garda, it is docked where the caller said it would be."

"Can they bring him to us?" McGarrity asked.

"They should be able to round him up and bring him to us tomorrow."

McGarrity slumped forward and put his head in his hands. Dunne got up and started feeding the fire.

"And what do you think of the other part of what he told us? The part about the girl?"

Dunne stopped what he was doing and though he hesitated his answer was sure. "I'm glad I didn't meet our informant face to face, because if what he said was true I think he's a dreadful fellow and it would be damned hard to hide my disgust for him. And my disgust is not the important thing. It's getting Vox."

McGarrity finished the whiskey he had poured. He felt more gratitude than disgust and wondered if it was a sign of good sense or old age. He said, "You're like our Mr. Bryce. You've got a sentimental streak and it's wasted on a woman. Ah well, there's worse things, though I don't know what they might be. Don't worry the fire, Dunne. We've got a chance for a few hours sleep. Such an opportunity cannot be taken lightly. We may have none tomorrow."

Four

Bryce woke with his head on a dead arm. He rolled on his back and, with the help of one arm, moved the other, starting up the pins and needles of regained circulation. Mrs. Quinn, proprietor of the B&B where he had obtained his night's lodging, had kindly given him the back room, the big one, because he was the only guest and this room had the best view. Lying there, he could just see the sun leaking yellow all over Bantry Bay's blue. Bryce stepped out onto a stiff, low-nap carpet. Across the landing was the bathroom, where he bathed in a claw-foot tub of yellow water and washed his hair from a spout set too close to the rim for efficiency. Tape, silver as Christmas tinsel, sealed cracks in the linoleum. His room was equipped with a sink and a mirror, and while he shaved, the smell of bacon cooking snuck in through the crack under the door.

Behind the wheel of Joe's car, Bryce had been able to think more clearly, calculating Katharine's possible departure times, her probable destinations. She surely made it to Bantry, could have come as far as Glengarriff, might even have moved on to Killarney that same night. The road between Glengarriff and Killarney was a high mountain road, often cloud-shrouded and always an obstacle course of sheep. However, if Katharine's goal was to put some distance between the two of them, imperiling the lives of a few sheep or risking loss of limb at the bottom of a mountain wasn't going to stop her. Still, he had to be sure; or at least try to be as sure as circumstances would allow. On the edge of Glengarriff, he stopped at this roadside B&B, drawn in by the big, welcoming blue sign, and by the light in the front window indicating that at that late hour he'd not be getting anyone out of bed. Mrs. Quinn had been watching television, and after her orgy of late night programming, did not appear any too lively this morning.

Breakfast started out a stunningly quiet meal, presided over by the pope and John F. Kennedy, gazing down on him in effigy from the wall opposite his table. Mrs. Quinn, who was large, with untidy gray-streaked hair and the authority of a woman who was an expert in her field, delivered his cereal accompanied only by a terse good morning and a brief inquiry concerning his preference for coffee or tea. His choice was served directly and without any side dish of chatter. It took a concerted effort as she delivered his bacon and eggs and sausages to get beyond her reserve. He commented on the weather, asked after the morning news, complimented her on the tastiness of her brown bread, the beauty of his bedroom view; she warmed a little. But it was the subject of fish that finally brought out her field of expertise.

". . . lovely fishing right off the island out there. The lads down the road are out regular, making a good living. Fish has had the most terrible associations, you know. Famine food. Some won't touch it to this very day. This area was very hard hit, all along the west, usually a land o' so much. Timoleague, Bantry, Clonakilty, God help us—" as she spoke, her eyes rolled, as if the memory were fresh and not a recollection from her great-grandmother's day "—but there's nothing better than a bit o' smoked salmon and a Guinness, to my mind. Among foreigners especially, since they have no prejudice, it's been appreciated. And it's regaining some popularity among ourselves. O' course, 'twas a great worry when the oil spill of nineteen-seventy—"

From the oil spill, she went on to recount how the weather had defeated the French fleet the winter of 1796–97, no more than landing in Bantry Bay when they had to turn around and return to France, taking with them the recruits and the leadership in the person of Wolfe Tone that the uprising on shore was waiting for. Mrs. Quinn's field of expertise was her bay, and she slid back and forth between centuries easily. Lost in her history lesson, she was surprised to find herself sitting down and drinking a cup of tea Bryce had poured for her.

"Here I am, running on and on, when it's sure you've got places to be going. Business trip, did you say?"

Bryce hadn't said, but he smiled regretfully.

"Ah, sure, that's almost all we get this time o' year, is businessmen. Though there's been precious few of those, Irish or otherwise, this week." She stood, gathering up her cup and saucer.

"No Americans?"

"Haven't had someone from the United States in oh, let me think, since the end of October."

Bryce sighed, and Mrs. Quinn took it as a sign of homesickness. It was her experience that Americans abroad deep down always preferred the company of other Americans. But he'd been such pleasant company, and not a bad-looking lad, once you sat talking to him for a while, that she could find it in her heart to understand the desire for one of his own kind. A terrible thing it would be, to be alone in another country. Mrs. Quinn didn't like being alone, even in her own.

"Last Thursday week, we did have someone from your part of the world. A Canadian," she told him in an attempt to please. America and Canada were neighbors, after all, and having no inkling as to the distance between California and Canada, she thought he might find this comforting. Bryce smiled sadly, and there was something in the sadness that compelled her to try again. Employing the principle that hearing the trials of others was a salve to your own, she said, "Funny, the Canadian, I mean. Not near so pleasant as yourself. Not doing well at all, in my opinion."

"No?"

Encouraged by his apparent interest and lack of hurry, she shook her head. "No. Troubled sort of person. Talking to the mirror, making the bed, unmaking it again. I tried showing a bit o' kindness, thought I might draw out the trouble, but I might not have been there at all for all the notice I got! Didn't eat but a bite o' breakfast! I mightn't have bothered cooking. Felt quite put out by it all, I did."

Bryce was sympathetic, making a remark concerning

the quality of the food that didn't feel at all like flattery
to Mrs. Quinn.

"Hate to see the waste of food, excellent or not," said
Mrs. Quinn, wagging her head.

A kindred spirit, Bryce agreed.

"Sometimes when you travel alone, you forget other
people are susceptible to your moods. Maybe it's getting
waited on all the time that makes you selfish. It allows
you to start thinking of people as if they were part of the
furnishings," Bryce said, and picked up his cup of tea
in such a way as to take a discreet look at his watch.

"Sure, it's not something I'll be getting the chance to
know. Maybe it's true for a man," conceded Mrs. Quinn,
not without a begrudging indulgence, "but you'd think a
woman would have more understanding."

Bryce tapped a spoon lightly against the place mat.

"The Canadian was a woman? Do you get many
women traveling alone, especially this time of year?"

"No, they usually come in pairs. But this one could
have used a keeper, if you be asking me. Gave her the
same room you have—like you, she was the only guest—
and asked her how she was enjoying the view, and she
looked at me as if she had no idea what I was talking
about." Mrs. Quinn was obviously peeved her bay had
been wasted on such a philistine.

"Then she couldn't have been a tourist. No tourist
would have overlooked that view," Bryce told her.
"Was she very young? Natural beauty, if it isn't in the
form of the opposite sex, is sometimes lost on them."

"True enough," she said with a sigh tinged with nostalgia, and perhaps with worry. (One of her sons had
been out late the night before; that was what had been
keeping her in front of the television.) But then she stated
more firmly, "She wasn't *that* young. Very polished-
looking. Could have been a businesswoman, I'm guessing. Though it didn't seem quite the right kind of polish.
And I'm telling you, if that's what traveling on business
does to a woman, she should be staying home."

Bryce sat absolutely still for a moment.

"You say she was talking into a mirror. What sort of
things did she say?"

"I'm no eavesdropper," said Mrs. Quinn.

"Oh, no, I wouldn't have dreamed you were. Still, you're dealing with the public, in your own home, no less. You have to be observant in the best interests of your establishment."

Such a deep, gentle voice he had. Appeased, Mrs. Quinn sat down again and told him, "Well, I was passing by, taking fresh linen into the upstairs convenience, and her door wasn't completely closed, so I could hear her. Thought she might have somebody in her room, at first, I did—gave me quite a turn. Can't be having those sorts of goings-on here, no indeed. So I took a peek round the corner. And there she was standing before the mirror doing the most peculiar—well, I wasn't sure what to make of it all." Mrs. Quinn leaned forward and lowered her voice, though they were the only two in the room. "Counting, she was. Counting her face. Takin' her thumb and like—I don't know how to say it."

"Show me," Bryce suggested persuasively.

Mrs. Quinn, inspired by a curiosity that surely matched her own, stuck out her chin, took her thumb and drew an invisible line down the center of her face, then a series angling off to the side, saying, "One. Two. Three. X. Four. X." Mrs. Quinn put her hands down awkwardly, suddenly self-conscious at such a show. "Some kind of beauty routine, I was thinking, seeing the creams and pencils spread out along the sink. She looked the type. Conceited."

"But?"

"But when I came back out of the convenience, I could still hear her going on, and so I had myself another look." Mrs. Quinn sat back and put her hands on her knees. "She'd just finished making up the bed. And I must tell you, I felt insulted—what did she think? That we don't change the sheets after they've been used? Did she think we were dirty? I was ready to tell her a thing or two when she started swearing like I haven't heard since Mr. Quinn died four years ago. And then she started ripping the whole thing apart again. Fierce, she was. *Fierce.*"

Bryce raised his eybrows. "Very strange behavior," he said.

Mrs. Quinn was on the roll; the more she thought, the stranger it all became.

"She looked half-dead when she came in the night

before. Sent her down to the hotel for a proper meal, I did. But come to find out later when I talked to Mrs. Mullins, who runs the pub there, that she ordered a round of smoked salmon sandwiches, then hardly touched them. Didn't even drink any more than one hot whiskey, so *that* wasn't her problem. Didn't speak to anyone other than Mrs. Mullins. Though Mrs. Mullins had a whole line o' regulars at the bar, every one o' the lads stopped and stared when she walked in.''

"None of them approached her?"

Mrs. Quinn snorted derisively.

"There's not an ounce o' action in the lot of *them*. Lookin' and whisperin's all they're good for. And this woman gave them no encouragement. Sat down by the window and stared out it the whole time, though there was nothing to see but the dark o' night. No talkin', no eatin', no seein', it was all very peculiar.''

"What part of Canada did she say she was from?" he asked.

"Oh, she never did. But I knew she was from Canada because of her accent. It wasn't like yours, although she had the flat A. No, it was more clipped, like she was a Brit, but not quite clipped enough, if you know my meaning. I know my accents,'' she told him, again asserting her authority, ''I've had them all through here.'' Mrs. Quinn started stacking his dishes with her own cup and saucer. "I'll be telling you. I told her 'safe journey' as she was leaving, same as I do all who leaves here, but I didn't believe a word of it.''

"One . . . two . . . X . . .''

"What are you doing?"

The reflection in the mirror had stilled instantly at his approach. They were getting ready for a party, a going away bash put on for him by his colleagues at the sheriff's department. He was aware of a tension, similar to that of the interrogation room, where his next approach could tip the scale for success or failure. His action was a stroke of inspiration that in retrospect seemed much more like James than himself. He'd taken the brush from her, tipped her chin and, after a moment of consideration, made a serious attempt to pick up where she left off. His ineptitude had amused her, his need for instruction had brought out the story of the ritual before the mirror. He envisioned a very young Katharine on a stool beside her mother, clothes taken from the closet still wrapped in department store plastic. Pots of creams, brushes, lipstick laid out meticulously as surgeon's scalpels. Preparing for a party her mother would take the time to explain Katharine's own face to her, carefully penciling the structure on the skin—a ticklish enterprise that set the both giggling. The spots where shadows should go were numbered (Katharine counting out loud), the spots where shadows ought *never* to go were x'ed. Blindfolded with a stocking Katharine had learned the difference in silks and wools and cotton in a guessing game that let her handle every item in her mother's well-chosen wardrobe.

This was the extent of their contact: the wardrobe games, the monologues on fashion that Katharine had looked forward to as any child might anticipate a bedtime story. Bryce saw a picture of the adult who did not know how to play with the child, the child who learned to play the adult. He had wondered briefly if her mother had had any girlfriends, and then remembering what James had told him of her wild reputation had thought it unlikely.

After that party Bryce had seen Katharine go through the count two times. Once before the London show and once before a much dreaded interview. He had come to understand it served the same function as nursery foods did for some or collecting Kate Greenaway books did for others. It was comfort, the response to a bare scrap of leftover affection.

Upstairs, he stood at the window. James had said she wasn't herself. That she might be someone other than herself hadn't seriously occurred to him. And if she wasn't herself then who was she? What was she? And what the hell was she doing? She was a decisive woman—had she become indecisive? confused? drifting? In need of a kind word—even as little as she trusted them? Could he get into her mind, the way he would get into a character, and find out what had happened to her? He did not have the resources of Special Branch, he could not follow Vox. But in following where Katharine would go he might stumble onto where she had been sidetracked.

Below, he could see a small strip of beach. The first time he had seen Katharine had been on a beach on Lake Tahoe. What had made him notice her was the way she carried herself; enjoying the sun, the water, marvellously indifferent to any attention she might attract. A couple of weeks before their parting they had visited a beach a few miles outside the village. Across the road was a hotel and pub that appeared shut down. Next to it a ramshackle park of small trailers, holiday homes for the people of Cork city, spread out some distance along the hills; all locked up tight. Bundled in their wool sweaters, they had watched two elderly couples shimmying out of their clothes under towels clutched ineffectively over sagging bosoms, balls, and bums. Where they had come from, Bryce didn't know. They had strolled around a bend of rock and there they were—no car parked nearby, all buildings apparently deserted. But unembarrassed, flashing old flesh, they squirmed into their suits, chatting with Katharine about the water. As they plunged in, Katharine stripped down to her underwear.

"They're a hundred and two if they're a day. If they can enjoy it, so can I," she had said.

"Katharine," he'd patiently advised, "when you're old, your sensory perceptions go. You can't taste, you can't smell, you can't see, and you probably can't feel your ass going numb because it's numb all the time."

"One day your chest will be all snowy hair and liver spots, and your prick will hang down below your knees."

"You should be so lucky."

Smiling, she'd looked out to sea. "And I'll have breasts to my navel."

"*I* should be so lucky."

She'd cocked an eyebrow at him. "Are you coming? Or are you afraid to test your perceptions?"

He only confirmed what he already knew. That the water was freezing, that the air was freezing, and that his prick would shrivel into nonexistence. Probably the purpose of the swim for these old gents—trying to shrink all bodily parts to a manageable size. The swim was short, and the men didn't last as long as the women, being almost dressed by the time those three rose out of the water. Katharine, between the two wrinkled and hunchbacked dames, stood more than head and shoulders taller. Firm-fleshed, goose-pimpled, and practically naked, she was laughing delightedly with her companion. Right then and there, he'd decided that when she was eighty, he'd still want to see her in a bikini. Just as she marched out of the water unselfconsciously, defiant of youth and the sensation it caused, so he would like to see her equally defiant of the creeping disintegration of age.

Yet for all her pleasure in life, she was a curiously easy woman to imagine dead. The same languidness that facilitated so much joy in little things also allowed a passivity toward disaster. Bryce rubbed his face with his hands, then watched a man row slowly across the water to the island.

If she wanted to leave the country, the most sensible thing to have done was take a car ferry. The closest one left from Cork. But he knew from the tightness in his own belly that she wouldn't head back toward the scene of the argument. Another ferry left from Dublin. If that's where she was going, she must pass through Limerick. *. . . wayward associates in Limerick . . . leaving a bit o' damage behind him . . . kneecapped a man in Limerick that afternoon . . . Can come and go as he likes . . . probably take a plane out of Shannon . . .*

Limerick, Limerick, Limerick.

Shit.

Five

James sniffed his sheets, then turned on his stomach and sniffed his pillowcases. In the fitful game of cat and mouse he had played with sleep, he had taken for a dream what was reality. He hooked his arms under the pillow and breathed deep. Recognized for what it was, the perfume became doubly potent, so that he was forced to question a state of mind that had allowed him to pretend it hadn't been there all along. The realization that it hadn't been *just* his state of mind, but also a bottle of Riojas consumed at a nearby pub before retiring, was not reassuring. Unlike Papa Bear, he knew who had been sleeping in his bed. It could be no other. Katharine was the only woman who had the key to his flat, the only woman he knew who wore that particular French fragrance, the only woman he knew who would appropriate his bed without changing the sheets.

He switched on the bedside lamp and blinked against the glare. Stepping, over his pile of discarded clothing and a duffel bag, he opened his closet. It contained only his own personal bits and pieces. In the bathroom he found a lipstick lodged behind the toilet, but how long it had been there, much less whose it was, was impossible to judge. He padded down from the bedroom loft into the living area. There was little to see. This was a place where people came and went, not where they stayed. He had once stopped escorting a woman intent on "decorating" his pied-à-terre, and had never regretted the decision. Four unmatched straight-back chairs of questionable ancestry and an aged pine table displaying a variety of spirits were set up before a hearth. The kitchen was tiny, hardly useful for more than making tea and sandwiches. He looked in the refrigerator, which seemed pointless since he had no idea what was there in the first place. His only noteworthy discovery was a slice of penicillin-coated pâté, which he stuffed hastily back in the cheese compartment. Except for the usual brown cracks in the porcelain, the cooker was clean. He paused before the sink, then touched its bottom experimentally, as if assuring himself it bereft of dirty dishes. In the cool night chill, he began to sweat.

The phone was set up on the table, next to a pile of darts. James sat down and stared at it. If she should walk in now, she would find him sitting in his underwear, freezing. She would see he had no inclination to play the role of negotiator, nor even that detached sympathetic friend, that he had changed. And that despite this change, he was sitting in front of the phone like a young girl plucking petals off a daisy. Love, love not. Call, call not. He picked up the darts. On the notepad beneath them was scrawled a set of numbers that were not dart scores. The time was inching close to three in the morning, but he dialed them anyway. He listened to the recorded message and then hung up. Sitting back, he took a dart and threw it at the dartboard hung above the elegant oak mantel.

Bull's-eye.

Six

Limerick was a nightmare of garda checkpoints. A smoky blue haze layered the city, lent the air the smell of burnt rubber. One long line of traffic crawled into town like a dog on its belly, past blue-suited garda and men in army fatigues toting machine guns. As a first glimpse of Ireland, this would be no comforting sight to a holiday-seeker, even had it been explained to him that it was all for just one man. The Ireland Tourist Board was probably on its knees thanking God it wasn't the tourist season.

Bryce took the presence of the garda for granted, too caught up in his mental pursuit to notice delays in the physical one. He had spent the miles between Glengarriff and Limerick trying to feel out Katharine's state of mind. When he had come home that first night to an organized home, he had interpreted its order in terms of clear, cold action; a reflection of his own brand of rational behavior. But the observations of Mrs. Quinn, having placed her conduct in a different light, put her where she ought to be in the realm of instinct. He felt her restlessness now as the panic of a cornered animal, her decision as frenzy.

Suppose, like a homing pigeon, she headed toward her most familiar mode of escape. An airport. Where would she go? London turned up increasingly in her conversation at this time of year. Something to do with the onset of Christmas, the feeling she was deprived if she was not in London for some part of it. In his opinion, this was the result of a yearly reading of *A Christmas Carol*. London was a place where she would not use the car, preferring in cities the use of public transportation. *Then what did she plan on doing about the Renault?* His first thought was, probably nothing. Logic intervened: she was careless, but not irresponsible. Perhaps she didn't intend to be irresponsible but had been prevented from leaving a message at Joe's, their usual answering service. Suppose Joe had been right. Special Branch was convinced Vox was on his way to Dublin; the airport might have been neglected but he doubted that. But Vox had gotten into the country; he could probably get out. Then why was the car found outside of Limerick?

He could argue with himself all day, waste hours checking every pub, hotel, and B&B in Limerick to justify doing what instinct dictated, or he could head toward Shannon.

Like most airports, the architecture of Shannon Airport exhibits all the drab confinement of a high school classroom. It is conveniently small, surprisingly so for the last European outpost. Inside, he hesitated, unsure of his next move. He was handed a flyer asking if his luggage had been out of his possession in the last twelve hours. He read it, looked up, and knew instantly his next course of action. In much the same way he found the B&B, he picked an airline. Very simply, the one having the most eye-catching sign. He waited his turn in the queue, then approached the counter and told the young woman there that he wished to see whoever was in charge. There was enough authority in Bryce's tone or a wild enough look in his eye, he wasn't sure which, for the woman went to fetch a supervisor without question. The man she brought was short, thin, and suspicious. Bryce smiled.

"I'm sorry to trouble you, but I need to check your passenger lists from last Friday and Saturday. If you call this number—" Bryce handed him the Dublin Castle card Dunn had given him "— you'll get the authorization you need to give me that information."

Bryce was escorted into a room accompanied by an uncommonly alert security guard. Fifteen minutes passed, spent in prayer and supplication begging Dublin Castle to back him up. At the end of this time, the man returned, holding in hand a computer printout and respectfully forcing on Bryce a cup of sickly sweet tea.

Bryce studied the printout and found that last Saturday at 9:45 A.M., Katharine Craig left Shannon for Heathrow.

James let the phone ring fifteen times before he answered.

Bryce said, "I apologize."

James countered with "What is it you want?"

Bryce paused significantly. "I know I was wrong."

"Yes. Apology accepted," James told him dutifully. "Now, that brings us back to my original question. What is it you want?"

Bryce ground his teeth, then laughed softly. "I don't suppose I can cry unfair, can I?"

"No."

"Then I should answer your question. Is Katharine there?"

"Not now."

"But she was," Bryce said quickly. "Did you talk to her?"

"She was gone by the time I got here, leaving behind dirty sheets, a clean sink, and a phone number." As if reminded, the phone paused to refresh itself with coin, dinging merrily.

"What phone number?"

"It goes to a Dublin commuter airline."

"Dublin?"

"Yes, Dublin. Crawling on her hands and knees back to you is my guess. You should be pleased," James observed neutrally.

"Then why Dublin and not Cork?"

"No one said crawling came to her easily."

"James . . . can you tell if she was there alone?"

"What?" Insult carried across the lines clear as a whistle-blow.

"It's a long story—" Bryce's sigh was lengthy, his depression effectively communicated "—and I'm running out of coin. But you may have been right, something might have happened."

"She's done such a good job of cleaning up, I have no way of knowing if she had company." James's voice sounded farther away than London. "What do you want me to do?"

Metered by the coin slot, Bryce thought quickly. "Call every hotel and B&B in Dublin and see if you can find her."

"Done."

"And, James, I hope—"

Bryce's hopes were left unexpressed. The phone beeped angrily and died with a wail.

Outside the terminal, Bryce was greeted by two stern members of the Garda Siochana.

"Mr. Bryce, we've instruction to bring you along with us. Would you mind giving the keys to your little car to us? We'll give it to one o' the lads to drive."

Bryce gave them the keys. He didn't suppose it would matter if he minded or not.

Seven

Mick Cronin arrived at Barry's Pub at precisely the same time every evening except Saturday, when he arrived a bit later, and Sunday, when he arrived a little earlier. The hour was a hangover from his working days at Guinness, as if he were keeping up appearances, although everyone knew he no longer worked there. Liam always arrived late, too ready to stop for a chat to be much of a man for a schedule.

"Hello, Mick. Did you order me up a pint?"

"Didn't know when you'd be coming, Liam. I never do anymore."

In the days since Liam's solitary truancy, Mick had never failed to remind him how sorely he'd been let down by his absence. Liam passed off the rebuke good-humoredly.

"Carmel," he said, flagging one of the barmaids. "Fix me up a pint, will you, love?" She gave him a nod as she passed, carrying a tray of drinks.

Liam turned back to Mick. Mick had a tendency to lecture, to pout, these days, and Liam thought it best to get the question out quick, though he could look at Mick and know the answer. But Mick seemed to want to be asked, to enjoy Liam's few words of comfort. Besides, they'd never get on with a decent chat until they got it out of the way.

"Did you get a letter today, Mick?"

"No. Nary a word. Silent as the grave." Mick stared gloomily into his whiskey.

Liam wagged a finger at him. "Now, don't be getting sour on me, Mick. She'll be writing you soon, telling you what plane she'll be on. You'll be having a warm Christmas, that's for certain, Mick."

"Ah, I don't know, Liam. Women are different these days. You're a lucky man, married so many years to the same good woman."

Mick didn't hide his envy, and Liam wasn't going to argue. He had been married many years, the woman was good, they'd had five children, and they'd been happy except for the times when drink or the bill collector had gotten the better of him. And there was Sean, though he went by that silly nickname now, making them both unhappy, but Nell especially. In the comfort of the pub where he hoped to forget his troubles, he could hear his Nell as he had the other night.

". . . Caught, I was. He was proud of me, you see, not leaving my family. Oh, he wanted me sure enough. But if I'd left with him, like he asked, he would never have trusted me. He would have thought me no good. He would have felt guilty. Funny, when you think of it. He could kill a man without thinking twice, but he couldn't love a woman and not take her whole history into account."

"I'd never try to make you feel bad, Nell, or make you stay if you hadn't the heart for it."

"No," she said, "that you never would have done."

And he couldn't tell if she was glad of this or not. But he had no complaints toward his Nell. Had none about his lot in life, either. Unlike poor Mick. Rotten luck, he had. Liam glanced around, recognizing faces, giving a greeting here and there. A busy night tonight. They were sitting at the bar, where it was easy to get the barmaid's attention. Carmel was setting up his Guinness. She was a pretty girl of twenty-two with dark brown hair and a smart way of dressing. Since this pub was in the Ballsbridge district not far from the American embassy, there were always a lot of posh-looking young people about. It was nice to see, made the world seem prosperous to

Liam. Waiting for the beer to make its second head, Carmel was talking to Annie Murphy.

"Nine hundred quid, they were asking. I could hardly believe it," Carmel said.

"Nine hundred quid!" Annie was a quiet woman, a mother of four whose children were nearly grown. Her face and body were worn thin, and on her upper lip a few sparse whiskers sprouted weedily. Always accompanied by her husband, she came to the pub for a whiskey and a little socializing. She was greatly shocked by the figure Carmel named. "That's very dear. Are you going to buy it, Carmel?"

"What's this we hear, Carmel?" Mick asked, interrupting them. "What will you be spending all that money for?"

"I've been looking for a leather skirt and matching jacket—"

"Jaysus! You're not going to be spending all that money for that, are you, girl? Would you be getting full value for money?"

"You've got to pay for quality these days," Annie spoke up, quick to defend Carmel's intention, though she knew little about quality except she couldn't afford it. Her husband handled the money, and all her clothes came from Dunnes or Roches. But she was obviously thrilled by the idea of so much money spent for so selfish a purpose. "And she's earning her own money, isn't she?"

Mick was trying hard to work up approval. "That she does. And she's a hard worker."

Liam said, "So when do we get to see this posh outfit, Carmel? You'll be breaking all the lads' hearts, including our own."

"You aren't going to be seeing that one," she said, serving his Guinness. "My sister's got a chum who can get me the leather wholesale. And my cousin knows a couple of Dutch ladies here in Dublin. If I give them my measurements, they'll make it up for me custom. The leather will cost about a hundred and fifty quid, and the work about a hundred."

Approval came easier to Mick this time. "Well, aren't you something? This is a girl with a head on her shoulders."

"But will ye be happy with it?" Annie wanted to know, perhaps a little let down.

"Of course I will. Designed it myself, I did."

Annie was duly impressed, fully restored; her watery blue eyes even shone a bit. "Well, aren't you something?"

Carmel served Mick another Paddy.

"Here now, I didn't ask for this."

"Here now," she told him, "you would in a second. I know your habits by now, don't I? You'll be waiting for me to be juggling a half a dozen orders and then you'll snap, *Carmel, I'm in desperate need of a refresher*."

They were all laughing when Liam said, "You're a smart girl, Carmel. A girl with a future."

"Sure she is," said Mick. "A nice-looking girl like yourself should be taken care of, Carmel. Get one of these posh lads from the embassy to take you to America."

"I could go to America without one, I could." She flounced down to the other end of the bar to take an order.

"Sure she could," chorused Annie, who would not go anywhere without her husband.

"They're cracking down on the Irish in America. Don't want us immigrating anymore," Mick said, deeply troubled. "Another case of oppression."

Liam knew Mick had never once thought of immigrating. He'd started young at Guinness and had a good job there for years, so there'd never been a need, as there had been with so many others, for him to consider a new home. It seemed he could make anything a personal issue for self-pity anymore. Couldn't help it, Liam supposed. He'd had such rotten luck. First his marriage, then his illness, which made it necessary for him to leave Guinness, then that liquor investment with his brother where the accounts hadn't tallied properly, and then his girlfriend getting a job that took her to Saudi Arabia, of all places. It was trying for a man.

"Ah, well, Mick, Carmel will do all right for herself."

Mick grunted ambiguously, his eyes straying around the pub. Carmel was being sassy with a group of lads at a corner booth. Three women sat before the fire, eyeing the men at a nearby table and whispering amongst themselves. A lone woman, no longer young, was striking up a conversation with a young man Mick knew to be a baker at the bakery around the corner. The baker didn't seem to mind the attention. No, not at all. His pale, freckled face seemed pinker than usual, and he was smiling, though he hadn't been drinking long enough to start doing that yet. Mick's eyes passed over the middle-aged couples, the lone and possibly lonesome men guzzling their pints. His attention was captured by a pretty woman wearing a beige storm coat. She strode purposefully past the bar to the back table, where Tommy, the pub owner, was sitting with his wife and friends. When Carmel saw her, she shot a look to the barman, who in turn relayed the gesture to another barmaid. The three of them started after the storm-coated woman, moving slowly but in such a way that Mick was made nervous and excited. The woman stopped before Tommy's table and peeled off the coat.

"Liam, what the bloody hell—"

She wore a pair of black leather shorts, a matching brassiere, and fishnet stockings. Brandishing a whip, she sang a silly, risqué little song wishing Tommy a happy birthday. Hooting, hollering, and gawking customers stood on tables and chairs, screamed their approval when Tommy sat her down on his knee, giving her a rambunctious, beer-lubricated kiss. She struggled and had just about made good her escape when Tommy, just for luck, pinned her again, taking more than his share of liberties.

On her escape, there was a determined gleam in her eye. Gingerly fingering the whip, she said, "Stand up, love. Bend over. Time for your birthday spanking."

On the first blow to his bum, Tommy's smile grew bleak; on the second, it went limp.

"There now, how does it feel to be at my mercy?" she asked him.

" 'Tis a fine thing," he croaked, sportsmanlike, "but you won't be going through all thirty-nine, will you?"

"Thirty-nine! 'Tis forty if it's a day. Naughty lad." And with that, she gave him a last solid nip in the tail with her whip.

The entire pub applauded. Tommy's wife, sipping gin beside him throughout the performance, smiled sweetly. Mick turned to Liam. "Well!" he said.

"She has a fine hand with the whip, doesn't she?" Liam stated thoughtfully, yet with a certain unspecified admiration.

"Tommy'll have himself a fine bloody bum!"

Carmel was back behind the bar in time for this last remark. "And no more than he deserves!" she said.

Mick looked surprised. "Deserves?" he repeated, mystified. Mick worked within a limited scope of imagination. If the girl dressed like a tart, then a tart she must be. Carmel was getting heated.

"She's a friend of mine. Goes to Trinity College and works sometimes singing songs for hire for one of these companies that send people out for a joke—you know, with balloons or in a gorilla costume, something silly for a lark. We hired her because Tommy's had this running joke with his wife ever since they saw some spicy movie when they were last in America. So us behind the bar here chipped in and hired Maggie to dress like that and sing a song we made up—*but did you see the bloody beggar?*"

"Aye, well, dressed like she was . . . and you have to make allowances—he had a bit o' drink in him, Carmel," Mick admonished her primly.

"A bit o' drink! That's a fine thing! He knows Maggie—knows what she is and what she isn't."

"I believe Maggie did get his attention and gave him his comeuppance," Liam said, kindly. "He won't be forgettin' himself again with her even if she came struttin' in stark naked.''

Carmel flashed him a smile of powerful beauty. ''That he won't. He'll not be sitting either, not in the next week,'' she said, resuming her barmaid's chores.

Licking whiskey off his lips, Mick whispered to Liam, ''Do you suppose she liked doing that? With the whip, I mean? She seemed to be enjoying herself.''

''I think she enjoyed giving tit for tat,'' Liam said, though he knew very well what Mick meant.

Four children and a husband had made it necessary for Annie to develop some very sharp ears. She heard Mick and Liam and offered her opinion with less than her usual tentativeness. ''It's not often enough the opportunity comes to let a man know how you feel about a predicament, and do it in such a way that you're sure you have his attention. It's bound to give you a great deal of pleasure when the impossible happens.''

Liam chuckled and took a pull on his pint, as much amused by Mick's aggrieved expression as he was by Annie's staunch observation.

''Well,'' Mick gasped, ''it's always fine to have a woman's point o' view.''

''O' course,'' Annie went on seriously, ''this entertainment goes too far for my taste. I can't say I approve of a young lady dressing up like that. Doesn't seem fitting.''

Liam said, ''Come on, Annie, it was just a bit of fun.''

''Sure,'' said Mick, ''it wasn't anything.'' But he looked furtively over his shoulder as if, indeed, it had been something. ''You know the situation. These young people work in Dublin, but most of them probably come from somewhere like Ennis or Tralee or Kenmare—small places with not a lot going on, where everybody knows your business. When they come to Dublin, it's the first time they've had any kind o' freedom or privacy. Can't blame them if they want to sow their wild oats.'' In the mirror behind the bar, Mick caught sight of himself and shakily adjusted his tie. His hand passed over his hair, leaving it a little better arranged. ''A lot of them even go home at the end of the week, come back on Monday. But while they're here, they can do as they please— nobody need know as long as they're halfway careful. Gives them the chance to enjoy themselves before they settle down. They could very well get tied up the way I did—you know my story, Annie." (Liam sighed, knowing they were to hear it again.) "I had a good job, so I married younger than most, as an inexperienced lad. And how long did it last? We lived for three years as man and wife though we've been married now twenty years. I'd like to marry my lady friend, but I can't get a divorce here in Ireland. I'd like to have children, but she won't— and can I blame her? No. And my case is not so unusual. You know that yourself well enough."

Annie nodded quickly and would have spoken, but Mick kept talking. He gave a jerk of his head toward a rosy-cheeked young man wearing a very well cut gray overcoat and a red silk scarf about his neck. He stood at the end of the bar, a hot whiskey in hand, telling a joke to a circle of appreciative friends.

"Look at that lad. He's got the world at his feet. They'll be no boring evenings for him, I can tell you; he'll be seein' the world." Mick's face was flushed, his nostrils pinched white.

Liam couldn't argue with the facts Mick was stating, but he was disturbed by the feeling behind the words. It was almost as if Mick was interested in being a young lout again. The feeling hit him not as a sweet wave of nostalgia, but with a bitter smell of unattainable desire. As if youth were the ultimate possession and Mick was furious his had been taken without his ever realizing what he'd possessed. Mick had been such a handsome lad when he was younger. Still was, in his way. But there was something about him, maybe this streak of self-pity—but no, Liam decided, self-pity was practically a national disease. Maybe it was that Mick lacked a sense of humor, unusual in an Irishman, and that was what made him less popular with the ladies. Without humor, the frustrations of Mick's life had soiled the fabric of his spirit.

Liam's frustrations had been soothed and sheltered by his wife and by the love of his daughters even though his son was most certainly a disappointment. But Mick had no such security, and he was no longer young enough to compete with lads like the ones in this pub. Liam hoped with all his heart Mick's girl would be home for Christmas, give him what love she could. Liam raised his glass.

"Here's to the younger generation. May they not get caught in the same traps we were."

"Sure enough," said Annie, raising a thin arm.

Mick shook his head. "Ireland changes slowly."

And Mick was no quickie either, Liam thought, losing some of his patience. Fortunately Annie, wise in the ways of changing mood and knowledgeable in the fine art of appeasement—God knows, she'd be dead by now if she weren't, for her husband had a quick temper and a hand to match—dug an elbow softly into Mick's ribs and jerked her head toward a woman at the far end of the bar.

"Ooo—she's giving you the eye, Mick. I think she's taken a fancy to you."

"No. You're having me on," he said. His flush deepened. He checked his appearance in the mirror before taking a surreptitious glance down the bar.

Always ready for a tease, quick to take Annie's lead, Liam said, "Don't underestimate yourself, Mick. She may be up for the game."

"Then she's no better than she ought to be," Mick said, suddenly reversing his opinion of the young.

Liam concluded, as he did more and more often lately, that Mick would be all right if it weren't for his vanity, his lack of humor, and his rotten luck.

Eight

Bryce was taken outside of Limerick to a house set far behind a high stone fence. It was dark when they arrived so he had no clear sense of the grounds except there were trees and clear spaces, no inkling as to how well they were kept or how deliberate their organization. They swung around a gravel parking lot, one surely too large for simply private use, and he was deposited, with escort, at the door of an eighteenth century manor house. The few cars in the lot and the faint glow behind a curtained downstairs window were the only suggestion of occupancy.

But Bryce soon found this deceptive. These thick walls did not give up their secrets easily. The front door opened into a wide foyer displaying the coat of arms, the banners and prizes, the usual paraphernalia of the landed gentry including that most contemporary addition, the ticket counter. It was manned by two unsmiling garda, one of whom jerked his head, signalling them on. They crossed the foyer. The second set of double doors they passed, opened and closed briefly, making Bryce aware of the urgent monitoring of more than one telephone. Then Inspector Dunne stood before them.

"Ah, you've brought us Mr. Bryce, have you," he said, addressing the garda, "I'll take him off your hands now. Thank you." The garda escort retired wordlessly, as if in this atmosphere he had absorbed the demeanor of minions past. Dunne looked at Bryce. "Come along. McGarrity's waiting," he said as if Bryce had been caught dawdling. He led him to yet another set of tall, double doors.

McGarrity sat at the end of a twenty-foot dining table and they had to walk the length of it to get to him. The chandelier above had made an early twentieth century conversion to electric light and its inefficiency lent a shadowed romance to a room that smelled of damp whose elaborately tooled wainscotting buckled like cheap wood wallpaneling. The family portraits were blighted by dirt and waterstains. Behind McGarrity was an enormous fireplace in the center of which burned a frugal turf fire. On the table in front of him lay a litter of papers, a coffee cup and a half a cheese sandwich on a chipped china plate. He rose from his chair, appearing to contemplate their arrival with patient disdain.

"Ah, Mr. Bryce," he said, "what do you think of our temporary accommodations here?"

Dunne handed McGarrity a set of papers then went to the fireplace to feed the fire. Bryce looked around, McGarrity seemed to require an answer. "They're depressing," he said.

"Do you think so? Perhaps it all depends on your point of view." He took a few steps, scanning the report Dunne had given him. Suddenly he tossed it among the rest and said, "The man who owns this house is an earl. He doesn't particularly care to be an earl, he'd much prefer being a fiddler in an American country western band. He may soon have his wish. As the literature out there on the counter will tell you this land was given to the family nearly three hundred years ago by the Crown of England. On the strength of that quirk in their family history from April to October they get a regular stream of curiosity seekers." He paused, considering the wainscoting for a moment before suddenly reaching out to put a finger to a loose edge. It was brittle enough to break at his touch. He smiled. Whatever McGarrity might be he was not sentimental about the possessions of generations past, or at any rate the possessions of earls past. "But tourist money cannot keep up with the creeping rot, Mr. Bryce, no more than police can keep up with the creeping rot of society. But, unlike the earl, we do have the occasional victory.''

Bryce's pulse quickened. ''Have you found Vox?''

McGarrity looked at him. ''Have you found your woman?''

Bryce checked the inclination to demand first things first. He gave a careful report of his meager facts and summed it up be telling McGarrity, ''It's all very inconclusive.''

''So it 'tis, so it 'tis,'' McGarrity said, but did not seem neccessarily displeased. ''You've done very quick work, Mr. Bryce. You didn't hesitate to use your contact with Dublin Castle and you didn't run crying to the press. I was told you had the knack and I believe it's true. Let me tell you what I also believe. I believe I have a bad feeling about you. I have the feeling, Mr. Bryce, that you could be a very big pain in my arse if you're not used correctly.''

''Then use me correctly,'' Bryce shot back coolly.

Eye to eye, he said, ''Oh, I think I have, Mr. Bryce. And I will continue to do so. On that I can give you my guarantee.'' He pulled out a chair. ''Have a seat.'' McGarrity sat at the head, Bryce on the left, Dunne on the right. ''Have you looked in the mirror lately, Mr. Bryce? If you did I'll tell what you'd see. You would see a man who looks as if he would like to take the entire world by the collar and shake until the teeth came rattling out of its head like tiny hailstones. You would see a man who made his woman so very anxious to leave him that she may have run straight into the clutches of a villain. A man who knows he may have set her up if not to be killed by Vox, then possibly by those seeking him. You would see a man who knows he's been sent out on a job the local law didn't want to be bothered with, who knows the safety of his woman is not their first priority. You would see a man in a hurry. You would see a man who looks at me with such anger I'm sure he would just as soon use his chair to smash my face as to sit on. What do you think of my vision so far, Mr. Bryce?''

''Twenty-twenty.''

McGarrity nodded, satisfied. "That fierceness can be put to better use than scaring the shit out of some poor girl at Aer Lingus."

"I was nice to her. I smiled," Bryce said.

"Jesus, Mary and Joseph," said McGarrity, "like some bloody psychopath. I have someone who might be able to give us our final link with Vox. I have coming in a piece of slime, Mr. Bryce. Specifically, a piece of American slime, a slime with no inclination to return to America. Five years ago he fled his country just as he was about to be charged with the embezzlement of a sum of $500,000 from his small accounting firm. Most of the money he lost in some ill-advised investments. He owes five years alimony and five years child support on four children. This is not a master criminal, Mr. Bryce, but a little weasel of a fellow who thinks his petty sins are the biggest in the world. A formerly respectable lad who thinks a term in jail would kill him. And well it might.

"These days he's got himself a boat and survives fishing and doing a bit of this, a bit of that. This is the first we've heard of any ill-doing. He had a small dose of Dunne earlier today, poor dunce tried to wiggle away from us, but odd as it may seem I think the threat of losing his carefree life by being extradited to the U.S. for prosecution would be a much more effective way of getting his cooperation."

"If he's in the country illegally can't you just tell him he'll be deported?"

"Ah, that's the low trick of it all. He's not in the country illegally. He's got an Irish passport. It's a privilege open to anyone who can prove they've had a grandmother born in Ireland, such as himself. And when he applied for it eight years ago he had no criminal record."

"So what do you want from me?"

"I want to demote you from the head of the CIA to a lowly officer of the American justice system. This has been his schedule so far, Mr. Bryce. We picked him up one hour, interrogated and beat the shit out of him the next, this hour we'd like to throw you and extradition in his face. I like the immediacy of it. He'll think we mean business. We're in a hurry and I want the dunce to believe his boney ass will be on the next plane to the U.S. to face the wife and trial, otherwise I might consider sending for a real officer, though God knows, his crimes being so petty I can't see you Americans being much concerned with bringing him home.'' McGarrity paused. ''I only want to put the fear of God in him and I think you could do that as well as anyone.''

''Do you have a report on him?''

McGarrity handed it over. Ten minutes later Bryce said, ''I'm ready whenever you are.''

Sammy Bean sat before them, a fidgety wiry man of forty, unable to put his back to the chair for the soreness of a small dose of Dunne applied to his kidneys. He had thin sandy hair and a thin sandy mustache on a red wind-eroded face. His hands were callouses, he had the nose of a drinker. He wore a sweater and jeans and waders. So natural did he look in the get-up that Bryce thought he must always have been sadly out of place in an accountant's office. He couldn't imagine anyone trusting him with funds. As if to give him a taste of the possible hell to come they had arranged his seat too close to the fire Dunne had got going, center stage to a cold circle of three. Bryce was introduced as ''the man come all the way here just to hold your hand on the flight home to the wife and family'' and kept conspicuously on his lap Sammy's file, a glaring reminder of past sins. From Sammy's chair there drifted the alluring aroma of wet wool, fish bait and fear.

''We know you've got your boat docked out of your usual area and we know you're supposed to take him out of the country. Now why not make life easier on the both of us and tell us all, lad.''

''You're trying to get me killed,'' whispered Sammy.

''Get you killed?'' questioned McGarrity. ''Now how can we be doing that if, as you were saying earlier, you don't know a fucking thing? You're confused, Sammy.''

''There's no confusion in me,'' said Sammy, and it was evident in the rhythm of his speech that he had made

major inroads into becoming more Irish than the Irish.
"You want me to betray Vox or go back to the States,
either way it's my life you're asking for."

"Let me introduce you to a more profitable line of
logic, Sammy. He can't get to you if we get him first."

Sammy snorted. "He's gotten away from you before,"
he said and glared as if his position in this business were
entirely McGarrity's fault.

But it was not in McGarrity's best interest to dwell on
the failures of the past. "That's because we've made the
mistake of trying to negotiate. It's not a mistake we intend
to repeat." McGarrity's grim sincerity got Sammy's full
attention. "Supposing you did take him wherever it is
he has a mind to go—do you think he's necessarily going
to repay kindness with kindness. You don't want the
opportunity to get on this lad's nerves."

"I know that. He's no hero to me," Sammy said
defiantly.

"If he's no hero to you and if, as I believe, you have
the power to help turn our luck around, then cooperate.
Unless, of course, you've got a hankering for a free trip
to the United States where you have a jail cell warming
for you with some nancy-boy, where the wife and children and former clients are all lined up waiting to welcome you back to their bosom." And while McGarrity's
words were farcical his attitude retained its grim aspect,
its aura of complete sincerity. Sammy wet his lips,
drummed his heel on the floor and looked at Bryce as if
the sight made him nauseous.

To show him his flat American A, to show him not a
man but a highly efficient duty-doer, Bryce stated baldy,
"If you want to negotiate with McGarrity, do it. If you
don't, as far as I'm concerned you don't have time to
pack."

"You can't—"

This pitiable delay tactic raised the hair on the back
of Bryce's neck. Sammy no more wanted to face Vox
than he did the United States. He knew it, McGarrity
knew it, Bryce knew it and Dunne knew it. Sammy had
only one risk worth taking if it was true that he loved

the life he had made for himself. He cut him short with, "We will."

Dunne had his eyes on Bryce as if he were the one who might require his restraining arm. McGarrity watched Sammy. Fire or no fire, Sammy had chills. McGarrity nodded once at Dunne. Dunne got out his pencil and notebook.

Sammy said, "Tomorrow night. I-I didn't know the passenger was going to be Vox. The story was . . ."

Book Three

One

In the Irish Tourist Board office at Dublin
Airport, Katharine thumbed through the B&B guide,
choosing one downtown, near the theaters. Behind the
counter, straight and alert as a sentry, stood a young
woman in a crisp ITB uniform. Katharine set her leather
satchel on the counter.

"I'd like to make a reservation here, please," she said,
pointing to the listing.

The woman touched Katharine's arm. "Mind your
bag, love," she said, and took the guide. She saw the
listing, then examined Katharine with an air of disapproval, as if she had made some terrible and naive error
in judgment. "You'll not be wanting to stay there," she
stated, certain beyond doubt or reason.

To say, *yes, I bloody well do*, was sure to sound rude
and argumentative. Instead, Katharine said, "I like to
be in the city center."

"'Tis easy enough to get to the city center," the sentry
said, as if that was a simple thing for any fool to see.
She glanced behind her, then leaned forward, lowering
her voice conspiratorially. "You're traveling on your
own? This place you're considerin' is *north of the Liffey*."

"Oh?"

The woman nodded vigorously, apparently sure she
could impart what the words *north of the Liffey* signified
by osmosis. She perused the listings, putting an author-
itative finger on another address.

"Here," she said, "this is where you'll be wanting to stay."

To Katharine, it appeared an innocuous address, without any special amenities, and the least of her concerns was what discomforts might await north of the Liffey. "I don't—"

The woman touched Katharine's arm again. "Why do you not mind your bag? You don't mind it, it'll be nicked by some rascal," she said, half-kindly, half-exasperated. Working in the tourist office, she was accustomed to giving unheeded advice. Katharine slipped the leather strap over her shoulder, and satisfied, the woman got quickly back to business.

"Ah sure, you'll love this place, you will," she said crisply, and picked up the phone.

A mixture of irritation, distraction, and plain fascination with the resoluteness of this commando kept Katharine speechless while her Dublin fate was decided for her.

After a short conversation, the woman hung up, obviously relieved. "That's grand, Fitzgerald house has a room." She filled out the forms while Katherine, to her own surprise, paid the deposit without protest. "'Tis a sure thing," said the woman, handing over the receipt, "nothing too bad can happen to you in Ballsbridge, if you're careful to mind your bag."

Katharine paid the cabbie. The guesthouse had no sign; it was just another Georgian doorway in a long line of brick residences; a half-moon of glass two centuries old over a massive white door, two columns framing it, a heavy knob direct center. The tiny yard was tidy. She liked the solid, austere look of the place.

Katharine was greeted by a soft-spoken man whose age she would have put at twenty by his appearance, twenty-three by his manner, and guessed was only seventeen. Everyone in this country looked older than their American counterparts. The house interior did not maintain the Georgian simplicity. In its heart it was a cozy, fussy Edwardian. The furniture was heavy and dark.

There were Staffordshire figurines, Belleek china, fringed and tasseled lampshades, and a sample of every crystal Ireland had to offer. Oriental rugs were piled atop other Oriental rugs, cushy wherever she stepped. Her room had an adjoining bath. She flopped down on a yellow satin duvet and stared at the coordinating wallpaper. This was a far cry from the Spartan residences of her single days, and she wasn't pleased. Of course, James's flat was not such a far cry from her single days, and she hadn't been pleased there either. She had suffered from the same scattered feeling she felt before beginning a new series of work. An inability to put the thread of her thoughts together, the quest for something that would make them whole. But she wasn't starting a new series; she just needed a change. A city she didn't know. She had been to Belfast several times with Kevin, but oddly, never to Dublin. She wanted a place with no memory.

The clock by the bed said four-thirty, but it felt later. She was hungry. Sometime lately she had consumed a ten-p bag of salt-and-vinegar crisps and a bottle of Ballygowan, but she couldn't quite remember when or where. The next time she looked at the clock, it was six twenty-five. She did not know where the time went since she did not feel rested. Eat, she told herself.

Downstairs, Katharine peeked into the parlor, then the dining room. They were both empty and there was no bell in sight, not even an encouraging light for the visitor. On the entry hall table was Dublin tourist literature, the newspapers, and a lamp. Feeling awkward and rather uncertain, she switched it on, and the click echoed in the deserted hall. It was cold. The floorboards creaked as she walked into the parlor, wondering when last the fireplace had been used, and loud voices began filtering up from the basement living quarters. Could there be fighting going on? What was she doing in this plush, unhappy place?

She opened the front door and rang the doorbell, then waited in the hall. The soft-spoken adolescent made an appearance a few moments later.

"That was me ringing the bell," she explained, "I

didn't know how else to get a hold of you."

"Ah, ringing the bell is just fine, miss. Whenever you like." He had a bland Dublin accent, with just enough music in it to mark it as Irish. "What is it you need, miss?"

Suddenly light-headed enough to faint, it took everything she had to say, "I'd like some instructions on how to get downtown. I'd like to take the bus rather than a taxi. And can you recommend a restaurant?"

"Go to the top of the road, miss, and catch the number ten bus. Remember that now, the number ten bus. Take you all the way—into St. Stephen's Green, Trinity College, O'Connell Street, whatever your preference. And there are many fine restaurants all over the city, miss. Everywhere, they are. Whatever suits your fancy."

Which told her he had probably never been to any himself. He handed her a brochure from the table.

"This has a small, simple map, miss, you might find helpful. Is there anything else?" he inquired.

He was attentive, polite, and impersonal. That was what she wanted, wasn't it?

"No," she said.

Before he left, he told her, "If I may make a suggestion, miss, I think you'd be very wise to mind your bag while you're downtown."

Upstairs, Katharine stuffed money into the various pockets of her jeans and leather jacket and left the bloody bag in the room.

In the Irish vernacular, "top o' the road" can be one of the most ambiguous phrases to be uttered to a foreigner. This time it was mercifully accurate. She rode on the top of the double-decker bus, because she found the improved view the best way to figure out the city's layout. Experiencing the peculiar clarity of mind hunger sometimes brings on, she sat through the route twice to learn the stops, studying the pocket map, feeling, for the first time in days, a sense of satisfaction. She was good at this. She folded the map and put it away.

The bus waited at a light. Directly ahead of them, also

waiting, was a horse pulling a flat bed cart piled high with plump green garbage bags. He was a sorry piebald, shaggy-coated and mud-spattered. The driver's ears were red from cold, and the sweater he wore, as muddy as his horse. By his side sat a young boy, head twisted to observe what was behind him. A pretty boy with long brown hair and a dirty face, his eyes seemed to meet Katharine's. She smiled. He turned away, indifferent rather than shy. The light changed, and Katharine looked down at her hands.

A second later, the clatter of hooves, a bellow, the thud of flesh hitting asphalt, brought her straight up in her seat as the horse fell, crossing the intersection. The driver jumped from the cart with an angry cry, grabbed the bridle as if with one arm he might lift the animal up off its knees. Startling as it had been to see something as big as the horse crumple into a heap, it chilled her to see in the beam of headlamps the face of the driver. Fiercely creased, frustrated beyond the problem of a falling horse, it was old not in years but in its place in time. His face was not modern, but a Hogarth engraving. Had the horse two broken legs, he would still make it stand, take that cart where it had to go. She was face-to-face with poverty, and it was not kind.

The horse was standing. The driver walked back to the cart to check its load. Anticipating abuse from the bus, the driver glanced belligerently its way and, in his scan of impatient faces, saw Katharine staring. He gave her what might have been meant as a smile but warred with the anger etched so deeply around his mouth, became the snaggle toothed leer of a gin-joint print. She'd heard it said that thatch reminded the Irish of poverty. If this was the poverty it reminded them of, it was no wonder to her so many had replaced quaint thatch with corrugated iron. She felt her fingers slide across the seat to take Kevin's hand.

She got off at the next stop.

Grafton Street was alive with artificial light. Streets in the shopping area were closed to autos. Pedestrians drifted undisturbed from one shopfront to the next, though it was too late to buy, staring wistfully at window displays. Or some marched quickly, elbowing their way to the nearest pub.

"Got a boyfriend, love?"

Katharine didn't acknowledge the man who asked but kept heading down the street as if she had somewhere to go. The elegant Brown Thomas department store had its Christmas decorations up already; so did Switzer's. She hiked on, hardly noticing the details, energized by so much light, so many colors, like a country hick on her first visit to the big city. She breathed it in, bent back her head to see the top of these short, spectacular buildings. Broadway could not have mesmerized her more.

She stopped outside Trinity College. Though it was late, a stream of students poured out from under the arch, like a tongue out of a dark mouth. Campus trees swayed in a gust of wind, leaves rattled around her feet. A paper bag sailed high, only to be impaled on the black iron pickets of the fence. Katharine turned abruptly and went back up Grafton then turned on a side street, almost running. The street grew narrow, the boutiques thinned. She must have passed a dozen restaurants. Irish stew advertised, Continental fare. She was fading in and out of hunger the way the desperately sick fade in and out of consciousness. She wanted a restaurant that would provide her with really good food, a truly warm atmosphere. She didn't want to make a mistake. She didn't want to be disappointed. Yet she hardly looked at the ones she passed, she read no posted menus. She turned into an alley that was narrower still and darker, its few restaurants more exotic. Chinese. Moroccan. Lebanese. Could they do well in this city? Dusted with a thin layer of coal smoke, there was a conformity to these old buildings, a strictness to the long line of flat fronts. A church steeple rose up, high above all. A shop window displayed a prayer bench, a sword, some rosary beads. Her eye was caught by a watercolor on the inside wall. An ostrich was dressed in the proud uniform of a military officer; stashed carelessly in his pocket was an opium pipe. She moved closer, but a sudden burst of loud laughter from the next-door pub spurred her on. She passed under an arch and arrived at Dame Street.

Like a seasoned Dubliner, she dashed out before traffic. A Fiat beeped at her angrily. She ran down an alley, stomach roaring. She knew she should stop, but this unnatural high-pitched energy, like the shrill sound of a shrewish woman, kept her going. She arrived on an unexpectedly crowded street, loaded with pubs. Fantastic young people, hair shaved or, if not shaved, wildly colored, their bodies lean, not a concession to fashion but a whiplash skinniness, ears stapled or safety-pinned, traipsed from pub to pub, mixed in with ordinary Dubliners.

A man stepped in front of her. "Got a boyfriend, love?"

She skipped up behind a stout middle-aged couple and followed them into a pub as if she belonged to their party.

Two

The last call for drinks, there was a crush at the bar. Katharine had bought a Guinness and was carefully easing away from the crowd. Not tarted up enough for tourists, this very plain pub with its plank seats and scuffed tables offered no cozy corners or booths. Though both sexes roamed freely through it, there was still the ghost of a divider where the women's-only snug used to be; the walls there, but the door removed. Katharine was about to park herself at a door-casing near the loo when she heard, "Without your boy-friend tonight, love?"

The voice was easily recognizable: husky, Anglo, world-weary. The woman to whom it belonged had violet eyes and a handsome face whose power was made more defined by the feather of lines at the eyes and mouth. Her salt-and-pepper-colored hair was cut very short. Sharp-shouldered and slender as any one of the punks outside, she was famous among her acquaintances for her appetite. Despite her size, it was enormous for both food and drink. For other, more subtle pleasures, she also had a reputation. Her published art criticisms were intellectual, acerbic, highly prejudiced, and amusing for those with a taste for blood. She did not suffer fools gladly, and her definition of fool was broad, encompassing nearly everyone who was either American or British. If Katharine was looking for a friendly face, it seemed unlikely she'd find it in Siobhan Riordan.

"I didn't think you were living in Dublin now, Siobhan."

"I don't know if I'd call being in Dublin living," she answered. Peering around the blue stem of her cigarette smoke, Siobhan watched Katharine closely. "You're looking very self-destructive this evening, Katie."

"Am I?" She took a drink of beer, twitching her nose behind the foam. Nobody ever called her Katie. Of all the variations of her name, it had to be the worst. "Still doing criticisms for the *Times*?"

"Oh, I've branched out. I'm leaving carnage all over the Continent and even in America now."

"How nice." Katharine frowned, feeling a need to concentrate.

"You disapprove, Katie? My dear, I believe you're going to fall flat on your face. I've never seen you drunk before. To be perfectly frank, it's always made me mistrust you."

"I'm sorry to disappoint you, Siobhan, but I'm not drunk. I haven't eaten, and my blood sugar's out of whack."

Siobhan threw back her head and roared with laughter. "Call it whatever you like, dear. One way or another, it does look as if you need food."

The barman struck a mean and commanding pose at the door. "Ladies and gentlemen, drink up, drink up. Time to close," he began, using an auctioneer's monotonous rhyme. No one paid any attention.

Siobhan gazed at Katharine speculatively. "Well," she said, finishing off the last of her whiskey, "unless you're absolutely determined to try one of our fine restaurants, I've some chicken curry at my flat you're more than welcome to—if you think you can make it as far as O'Connell Street for a taxi. You're twice my size. I can't carry you."

Katharine smiled bleakly. "You don't live north of the Liffey by any chance, do you, Siobhan?"

She replied with a puzzled "Yes."

It was Katharine's turn to laugh.

* * *

Katharine sidestepped a puddle of vomit. A little farther on, she jumped over the spread legs of a man lying unconscious on the pavement. They were hurrying down an alley lit by moonlight slipping through a break in the clouds. Katharine stopped, startled by a movement in a recessed doorway. A boy and a girl grunted against the brick, a glint of light shining off their bald heads, their black clothes and tight body-grind making one indistinguishable from the other. A single tuft of long white hair stood out of the center of the girl's small head, flung up and down in a private, personal rhythm. Katharine felt Siobhan beside her, bumping a shoulder against her arm.

"Didn't know you were such a voyeur, Katie."

Voyeur struck an oddly sensitive chord. She lashed out crisply, "I thought Ireland was supposed to be repressed."

"If it weren't, they'd have a proper place to do that sort of thing."

They moved on. Young men lurched down the street, shouting obscenities. An elderly gent put his back against a building and slid down to rest his rump on the sidewalk, farting juicily all the way.

Siobhan sighed and said, "Ah, there's nothing like Dublin at pub-closing time. There's a taxi."

Across the street was a group of concrete flats that reminded Katharine of low-cost housing she'd seen in San Francisco. Siobhan lived in a brick ghetto, older than the concrete counterparts by probably 150 years. The inside was dark and filthy. Springs hung out of chairs. Before the stove was a Turkish carpet, its pattern obscured by coal dust and dried mud. The room stank of mildew. The wood stairs were an unfinished construction job: scuffed, splintered, blotchy with stains. What few windows there were had never been washed, and the lace curtains were nicotine yellow. But on the walls— along the hall, down the stairs, in this pitiful receiving room and no doubt in the kitchen, bathroom, and bedroom as well—was a display of art. Quality art. *Brilliant* art. Oils. Watercolors. Engravings. Small sculptures.

Katharine recognized the work of many of the artists. There was even a sculpture of her own, an early work when she still came cheap. Cookbooks were piled on a table riddled with wood worm. Katharine was drinking an Alsatian wine. The aroma of chicken was determinedly overriding the house's less succulent odors. It was rare to see passion laid out so clearly. There was art and there was food; little else seemed to matter.

The bathroom was unspeakable. *Thank you, Siobhan, for introducing me to my first Irish crabs.* She laughed out loud.

"Katie, are you quite all right?"

Katharine came out of the bathroom smiling. "Don't worry, it's just my natural high spirits."

"I never realized you had any. Drink does do the most peculiar things to you." Katharine opened her mouth, about to protest, but Siobhan continued on, "Is it the Puritan strain in Americans that won't allow them to admit they're pissed?"

Katharine gave up. Siobhan returned to the kitchen, smiling smugly. At the coal stove, Katharine stood studying a watercolor on the opposing wall. In it a woman sat in a chair, naked except for an open shirt; breasts sagging, legs spread. Straight black hair drew down a face that though not old, was careworn, cruel. Yet vulnerability was there. She was tough, but perhaps not tough enough.

Siobhan came from the kitchen, carrying two plates of steaming rice and chicken. "Do you recognize her? It's Rodney Strong's paramour. Or was. She committed suicide this summer past, surprisingly enough."

"Why surprisingly?" Katharine asked.

"Because, my dear, it's not losers who commit suicide, it's perfectionists."

"You thought she was a loser?"

"Not much of an intellect there. I quite liked her personality, what little there was of it. Of course, she had marvelous tits, though you wouldn't know it from Rodney's portrait." She nudged Katharine with her arm and handed her a plate. "Never mind, Katie. You need something to eat. Sit down."

A part of Katharine wanted to believe that Siobhan was being genuinely pleasant. To offer food and wine to the needy seemed such rudimentary kindness. She tasted the chicken; it was very hot and delicious. Chewing slowly to take full advantage of the best meal she'd been offered in days, it seemed ungrateful, if not downright paranoid, to doubt Siobhan's motives. By the time Katharine had taken five well-savored bites, Siobhan had devoured her entire meal and was eyeing her indulgently.

"Do you know what I mean by perfectionist, Katie? Allow me to give you a little lecture. Consider it your mealtime entertainment. I mean someone who sets a very high standard for himself. Who is never satisfied, who pushes beyond what others regard as the normal limits. Of course, this person has no concept of normality and so has no idea how far he's stretched beyond it or of how unreasonable the next step he takes—the next expectation—might be. A person like this is bound to be impatient, to make the most remarkable accomplishments, all the while thinking he's only followed the usual course of events. With these, shall we say, unrealistic notions of life's possibilities, and driven by God only knows what demons, it seems inevitable that he will be disappointed by the world, but mostly by himself. Who can live up to their own standard? For most of us, that doesn't pose a problem—we don't give a shit. But this person lacks the complacency that makes for comfortable living. So disappointment, despite accomplishment, turns to despair. At some point the only way to battle the futility is to remove the object of it—namely himself. Suicide, you see." Siobhan paused delicately, smiled sweetly. "Personally, I've always thought you a prime candidate."

Katharine blinked, amazed by this bizarre left-handed compliment.

Siobhan hastened to add, "Of course, that was before I saw your exhibit in London last year."

Katharine sighed. The milk of human kindness had been offered only to fatten the lamb before slaughter.

She stabbed a piece of chicken and said, "It was a very popular show."

"I should think so. It was lovely." Siobhan laid her plate on the dirty floor and lit a cigarette. "It didn't have the rawness—the *edge*—of your earlier work, but there was a quality to it that would certainly have a . . . popular . . . appeal."

Katharine was too familiar with cruelty not to recognize the technique. The sugar-coated taunting. The laugh saying, of course, it didn't matter at all, as if by saying so, responsibility could be denied. The idea was for the victim to pay attention. Only once the desired effect had been achieved could a disclaimer be issued. When you relaxed, tried to trust, came the thrust of the knife.

"In the past, your art has always been of a type to hit right in the gut."

"It depends where your gut is placed, doesn't it? On your life's experience, what's going to hit the mark."

"Yes. Well. If before it came from your gut, my dear, now it seems centered a bit further down. That always has a following."

"It is the response that matters in artwork, it's not an intellectual field."

"Isn't it? Perhaps. Yet to use something as openly sensational as sex seems lazy, and your answer a platitude—an inchoate one at that," she said, apparently delighted at the conclusion.

Katharine didn't know if Siobhan really believed what she was saying, but the impulse to argue was for once overwhelming.

"Inchoate? I'm not sure it can be anything else. Perfection can't be expressed, only hinted. We have an awareness of perfection in our minds, and to get at it, you have to go beyond words into form. You can't rationalize it with technique. And if you do, you risk destroying the instinct. How many works have you seen ruined because someone got a deliberate *idea* in the middle of it?"

"Certainly none of yours."

Katharine let the remark pass. "In that painting over

there, suicide is articulated by the form. You don't need to talk to her, to listen to the banal details of her life story, to understand her feelings or know what she's going to do. There's nothing inchoate about that. But the artist who painted it had to trust his instincts, go beyond the rationalizations of everyday life to get at it. Consciously he might not have said she's going to slit her wrists—or whatever it was she did. She might still have been calmly bringing him his tea at four every afternoon—yet he was in touch with her feelings of despair.'' She wondered if she was making sense. She wondered if they had strayed from the original point. She wondered what the hell the original point had been. She wondered if there had been any point at all. She shut up.

"If it's all a matter of instinct, what happens when you have conflicting ones?" Siobhan asked.

"Then you're going to be cranky."

"Spoken like a true intellectual."

"Look, Siobhan. I'm very tired and don't like discussing art anyway. Could you have mercy on someone who hasn't had a very good day?"

"Katie, was I rude? I didn't mean to be. Knowing your famous reticence, I feel honored that you deign to speak of art at all. Of course, you must be very tired. Strain, no doubt." Her violet eyes were apologetic, though her face was as hard and careworn as the one in the portrait. "Tell me, are you still with that man you brought back from America?"

"I didn't realize you and Kevin had met," Katharine said, and made an unsuccessful jab at a piece of chutney.

"We most certainly did. At the reception. Had quite an interesting chat. Such a cultured voice he has, for brute force."

"Brute force?"

Siobhan continued smoothly, "I'd never seen your taste in men before. You've always been unusually discreet in these matters. Perhaps that's why I was surprised at your parading him about. After all . . ." Siobhan waved her hand, letting the sentence drift as airily as the smoke from her cigarette.

"After all, what?"

"Well, my dear, all men are beasts, and the police in particular are not noted for their intelligence."

Katharine sat back in her chair, felt a spring pricking her spine. "Is that all he told you about himself? That he was a policeman?"

"He didn't even tell me that much, someone else did. His topics were chiefly the weather and the visitor's guide to London. Why? Is there anything else to tell?" Siobhan contrived to look interested.

He writes some of the finest books you'll ever have the pleasure to read, Katharine wanted to say, but checked herself. It was a silly, defensive mistake she wouldn't have dreamed of making usually. Siobhan wouldn't care that Kevin wrote, much less the quality of what it was he produced. That wasn't the point of the conversation. One side of Katharine's mouth curled up. Kevin must have disliked Siobhan instantly to have restricted his conversation to weather and tourist sites.

"You can hardly say he was paraded, Siobhan. He was simply there," she said, and caught Siobhan glaring at her. This expression instantly dissolved into a kind of gentle reproach.

"He couldn't be missed—do eat, silly girl, don't let my admittedly prejudiced opinions spoil your appetite— why, you couldn't make a move without his eyes on you. You were virtually under surveillance. Ah, Katie, it was obvious from the show it's a very safe world you've entered."

Katharine's fork chased a bit of chicken across the plate.

"You're adored by a man who I presume is competent to protect you from the more primitive dangers of life. Your work sells well enough, I suppose? And not cheaply. But then, you've always had income to one degree or another—insurance, I heard. Your parents died young. So sad. Thank God you had money to cushion the blow—so many don't."

Katharine considered throwing the plate in Siobhan's face.

Siobhan sighed. "Ah, to be young, comfortably off, beautiful, and loved by all."

All too aware of the irony, Katharine whispered, "Not quite by all." Had her parents loved her? Probably. It had been so long ago, she couldn't remember. And they had died anyway. Her mother quickly, messily, drunkenly, in a car crash. Her father, sick with cancer, depressed at the loss of his wife, had hung himself in the basement. Could he have loved her and been inconsiderate enough to leave himself hanging where she found him? Or had medication or grief affected his reason? Had her uncle loved her? Maybe. He'd been considerate at least. But he had died too. That left her guardianship to his son, a much older cousin whose sharp teasing had escalated as years went by, beyond jokes, into cruelty. She didn't understand the word misogyny at thirteen, she simply thought she couldn't do anything right; and she hadn't understood the complex passion her cousin had for her mother. By eighteen she understood them both all too well. Had he loved her? Not in any usual sense, and he'd lived on for years. Was she loved now? It was too dangerous a proposition to contemplate.

"My God, has your boyfriend thrown you over? Is that why you're carousing drunkenly through the streets of Dublin?" Siobhan got up and refilled their wineglasses, an extravagant gesture considering the price of wine in Ireland. "I must say, Katie, you have a brilliant sense of style. If one is going to drown their sorrows, Dublin has a long tradition of that sort of thing."

"Really, Siobhan—"

Siobhan sat on the arm of Katharine's chair, sipping the wine in her glass while hugging the bottle close. "Drink is one of the most reliable sensual experiences life has to offer—much more reliable than men. Are you finally discovering that? How old are you, Katie?"

Katharine put her plate on the floor and picked up her wineglass. Siobhan placed a hand on her knee. "Don't worry, love. You'll soon find another. And another. And another. And probably another after that. Women with your physical presence always get by. But never mind me, dear. I mean it as a compliment.''

But Katharine did mind. She did not dislike her appearance, did not think of herself as too fat, too thin, too tall, too short, clear-skinned or speckle-faced. But any mention of her appearance made her uncomfortable, regarding it, at best, poor taste; at worst, hyperbole. She stood abruptly.

''Siobhan, I don't like being played with this way.''

Siobhan slid sideways into the chair, saying, ''Why are you attacking me! It's not my fault your lad's taken off.'' She coiled her legs into the seat, brought her chin up a fraction higher. ''And really, if you feel toyed with, why do you allow it?''

Katharine went down on her knees before Siobhan to make sure she had her attention.

''I've a fascination for this kind of arrogance. You see, I wouldn't find anything quite like it in the States. For sheer rudeness, no one can do better than the English, and it's obvious you've lived among them for a very long time.'' She looked down into her wineglass and slowly dipped her finger into the dregs to hide the effort it took to get these three sentences strung together, timing perfect. She heard Siobhan gasp:

''Nasty woman. I don't need the *English*—''

Katharine rubbed the wine on her finger onto the rim of her glass. ''I've matured from a silly girl into a nasty woman all in less than ten minutes time. What progress.''

''Don't be defensive, Katie—''

Forgetting herself, Katharine responded seriously.

''I'm not so much defensive as puzzled. I've been resented before, Siobhan. That's not original. But we had a real reason to hate one another. We were family, you see.''

Siobhan threw back her head and laughed. ''Brilliant. Absolutely brilliant . . . family, you see. Dare I say it? Could there be a true wit buried in you?''

Might as well leave Siobhan with the illusion she was witty. The clear, pale liquid in her glass grew fuzzy. She took a deep breath and it was like crystal once more. Siobhan reached out and brushed back a lock of hair fallen in Katharine's face. In a surprisingly tender move, she cuffed Katharine's chin with her finger, tipped her face upward.

"Silly me," she said softly, "I thought you might be crying. Should have known better. But you are unhappy. I'm not making any mistake there, am I? No. I didn't think so." Losing the crisp edge of her upper-class accent, her voice became lilting, smooth. She touched Katharine's dry cheek with her thumb, drew her face close enough for Katharine to catch the mixture of booze and curry on her breath, the dank scent of thirty years of cigarette smoke coming from her lungs. It was a peculiarly appealing odor—like that of horses or a beloved man's sweat. But then, Siobhan was a peculiar woman: powerful, changeable, experienced in both sides of pain. Katharine studied the lines of wear on her face the same way a palm reader might study the lifeline of a hand.

"Ah, Katharine, do you have a place to stay tonight? You didn't plan on sleeping in the streets, did you? There's no need when you can stay here."

If Katharine had any doubts as to the significance of the invitation, they were answered in the way Siobhan took the bottle, which she had kept close, took Katharine's glass, and set them on the floor. In the sweet way she took Katharine's hands into her own. Katharine couldn't help comparing Siobhan's physicality to Kevin's. Her hollow, caved-in chest to Kevin's solidness; the slight comfortable thickness of his waist to the exquisite angularity of her shoulders and hipbones. She also could not help comparing certain aspects of their character. She remembered her first morning with Kevin; she could imagine one with Siobhan.

"You see something, you abuse it, and then you want to fuck it. I'm not blaming you, Siobhan—it seems to be the way of the world. Or do women fuck each other? It's the kind of distinction that's always baffled me." Katharine took her hands away and retrieved her wineglass.

"You're a tease, Katharine." The tenor of Siobhan's voice changed, riding a tenuous line between defensiveness and flirtation.

Katharine looked at her for a moment before she said, "You're operating under the old male premise that a woman who consents to listen is a woman who consents."

"And doesn't she?"

"No."

Siobhan sat back, taking the bottle with her and drinking straight from it. "You don't appear outraged."

"Why should I?" Katharine laughed a little. "It's given me back my sense of the ridiculous. I've lived in Paris, London, New York, and San Francisco, but I had to come to Dublin to be propositioned by a lesbian."

Siobhan seemed to interpret this as an insult to her country. She responded with dangerous dryness, "We're not completely backward. We do have the usual range of human desires. Perhaps it's happened to you before and just gone over your head."

"That's possible," Katharine answered without irony. She finished her wine and stood, though part of her wanted to stay, perhaps preferring Siobhan's familiarity to strangers. "Thank you for the chicken, the wine, and the brush-up course in human nature."

"I can't call you a cab. I haven't a phone." Siobhan did not disguise her delight.

"I can walk."

"Through this neighborhood? Taxis don't cruise in Dublin. You'd have to make it clear to O'Connell Street. You must be mad."

"Stark, raving."

Siobhan didn't offer to escort her to the door, didn't say good-bye, didn't even whisper a final insinuation under her breath. She simply sucked greedily from her bottle, eyes closed. Katharine watched, aware of a creeping sense of horror; a vision of a life made up of small, reliable sensualities. Liquor, food, beautiful objects— simple, pleasurable, no hazard to the emotions. She wondered if the fear she felt was kin to the feeling a daughter might have looking into the face of her mother, seeing what could be, what was very likely to be. For reasons she knew Siobhan would perceive as weakness, she bent down and kissed the woman's cheek.

She stepped outside. Her usual appreciation for the sting of cold air, for the romance, the beauty, even the dingiest corners of a city offered in moonlight eluded her. At eighteen she had decided there was dignity in loneliness. In time the ideas had become synonymous in her mind, believing that in the distance created between people, one could never be foolish. Behind her she heard the creak of the door. Siobhan stood, swaying slightly in the breeze.

"You can always come back," she said, "if the dark starts to frighten you."

But Katharine knew this wasn't true.

Three

The post was late. A watched pot never boils, was Mick's involuntary thought. Maybe it was anticipation, maybe it was the effect of the wind kicking up, but Mick was restless. Dressed in his office finery, he set a brisk pace in the direction of St. Stephen's Green; was soon through it, past it, without much noticing its lawns and trees, its ponds and accompanying waterfowl. The clouds overhead were thick and dark, but the air was free of rain, so he used his umbrella—a distinguished one, a gift from Maire—like a walking stick, staking out his next step. As desensitized as a husband to an old wife's nagging, her disdainful sniffs, her intimate scents, so was Mick to Dublin's eccentricities. Once in a while he jerked at the sound of a horn, twitched his nose at a pungent odor. So intent was he on nothing that when he collided with a man on the street, he reacted not with his usual angry curse but simply gazed at him as if startled to discover he wasn't alone on the street.

The man was part of a group, all suited up, ties askew, their hands caught in gestures emphatic enough to indicate they had been discussing something important. No doubt on their way to the Shelbourne for a posh and significant lunch. Government. The wooing of badly needed big business. Bloody cheek. Deep below the surface, Mick felt his blood begin to boil.

All this group of men saw was a man dressed for business, his stride determined enough to suggest a destination, something obviously on his mind. So they acknowledged him, an excuse and a nod, a token of camaraderie that brought Mick up short. A rush—God, it had been so long!—of nostalgia for his part in the working force checked his irritation. No, he'd never been one of those lads on the dole, some of them never knowing anything else. No, he'd had his place. Not as posh as these gents, but work was work. He'd had his title, his identity with the company, his friends and workday conversation, his field of expertise. It could still be seen! His spirit swelled. He squared his shoulders and walked on; the kindly gent in his blue suit and handmade shirts, his silvery hair becomingly blown by the wind, carrying his very fine umbrella.

In front of Brown Thomas, he stopped to look at his watch and took the opportunity to check his appearance in the store window. Beyond his reflection he saw a mannequin dressed in the latest from a fashionable American designer. Very pretty, it was. He moved closer. His Maire'd look grand in it, though he'd never seen her in anything so flashy. She always wore a skirt, a blouse, a sweater, something modest. God, it must cost the earth, a sinful waste of funds, he thought, observing it sourly. Yet what a feeling it would be to . . . but no, it was something more likely to be seen on Carmel than Maire. He wet his lips. The thought of Carmel had kept him awake more than a few nights while Maire was gone— the way she sashayed around, showing it off. His eyes narrowed. What was it there? What was the pattern on the scarf? It was a big scarf, draped around the shoulders and knotted loosely in front. Beige and green, a touch of red and brown, a kind of hunting scene on the border. That's what it was! The middle was filled in with a lot of tiny riding crops. Made him think of the girl in the pub the night before. He shifted uneasily on his feet, smiled sheepishly. He'd been needing a present for Christmas, wouldn't he? Something classy for Maire. It would be perfectly respectable buying her the scarf, extravagant even. Maire'd appreciate the quality. It excited him, the idea of Maire wearing it. It was like having his own private joke, a fantasy. A bit of naughtiness. He should buy it for luck; an act of faith that she'd be coming home.

He stepped into the store, buoyed by the confidence given him by the men on the street. He was an accomplished man, going into a smart shop to buy a present for his mistress. He was a lover. He tugged at his shirt cuffs. Floors carpeted and wall darkly paneled, this section of the store was as hushed as a church and far better insulated against either noise or poverty. And like in church, he didn't feel completely at ease here. The only customer, Mick advanced to the counter, where there stood a saleswoman of about his own age, as impeccably turned out as any one of the mannequins. She interrupted her study of a printed sheet to smile at him, then returned to it. Inventory, Mick surmised knowledgeably. She had too much paint on her face for Mick's taste, and something about the vagueness of her smile rattled him, as though she hadn't given him proper consideration at all. Waving his hand, he demanded imperiously, ''That scarf in the window, would you have any more of them anywheres?''

She started. To his own ears, Mick sounded uncommonly loud.

''May I help you, sir?'' she said very quietly, setting the sound at the proper level.

The example was not totally lost on Mick, but embarrassment kept his voice not quite under control. ''The scarf in the window with the—'' he started to say *little whips*, but suddenly the words seemed not quite decent ''—the one in the window, the big one. Is it the only one you have?''

''I believe so. It's a fine blend of wool and silk, sir.''

''Well, o' course 'tis,'' he said, frowning. ''Wouldn't expect anything less.''

The saleslady did not appear convinced of his eye for quality. She tapped the top of the glass counter between them and said, ''We've a nice selection of other scarves in the counter. Smaller and quite lovely.''

Jutting out his chin, Mick perused the collection, seeing nothing that aroused his fancy the way the scarf in the window had. He dismissed them all, saying, "No. The one in the window, that's the one."

She made no move to fetch it for him. As he spoke, she was bringing out a couple of scarves from the counter and spreading them over the glass. They were delicate florals, hardly more than a wisp around the neck. What was wrong with the woman? Was she bloody deaf? Surely if he was firm, she'd be impressed by his authority.

"Did you not hear me, woman? I like the pattern of the one in the window!"

She stiffened, but other than that, blandly ignored the growing belligerence of his tone. "Ah," she said, "the hunting motif. I have one or two others. Let me show you—"

Mick could hardly contain his impatience. He glanced at the scarves, and saw that they, too, though larger than the last crop, were still smaller than the one in the window. It dawned on him that they might also be priced accordingly. Jesus, she didn't even think he could afford the fucking scarf! Angry and oddly confused, he blurted out, "But they haven't got the whips on them!"

She stared. He knew he was flushing clear to the roots. Her own color was high—even her eyes looked watery! She must see something smutty on his face, hear the guilt in his tone. Her lips were trembling as she said, "I'll get it for you." She hurried off.

It was his chance to slink out the door and never see the woman again. He took two steps, then stopped before a mannequin and reconsidered. If he left now, wouldn't she think he couldn't pay for the scarf? Wouldn't he be confirming the woman's worst suspicions? He pondered this for some time. His pride stirred. Hard as it might be, he could only brazen it out. Damn her delicacy, the old biddy! Nothing in the whips anyway. And even if there was, how could she know? He shifted his feet and gave a sly glance at the mannequin. It was dressed in garb similar to the one in the window, minus the scarf. What was taking the woman so long? For a second he felt a wave of panic. Maybe she had gone for the manager or a guard. But no, of course not, silly fool. There was a tag hanging from the mannequin's blouse. He fidgeted with his umbrella, taking a slow look around the boutique. No one was there. He reached out, turned over the tag, and gasped.

The saleslady was back before he could get to the door. She rang up a staggering though not impossible sum—after all, he saved his money—which he paid by check. She bagged the scarf and handed it over slowly; in Mick's opinion, as if she didn't want to give it over to him. "Thank you," she said, sniffing twice. "We don't usually sell things from out of the window. But it is a lovely purchase. I hope it brings you much pleasure."

He snatched the bag from her and left, tripping over the rug as he went.

Four

Dunne drove Bryce toward a place just west of Dublin where McGarrity was already hard at work. Clouds rolled in behind them, catching up quickly, passing with ease. The road stretched out, banked on either side with unremitting greenery. Old men wearing wool caps would appear at intervals by the roadside, walking greyhounds on a lead. Mongrels perched on gate pillars, proud and fierce as griffons. The family fortunes of the farms they passed were chronicled in their structural legacy—the stone fortress, a roofless skeleton, the Georgian farmhouse, the occasional cottage thrown in, once thatch now roofed with corrugated iron if roofed at all. The modern bungalow sprung up among these like a bud from a tree stump. These sights did not tick off miles as landmarks should but helped to render a sameness to the scene, as if they were merely running in place. Bryce glanced at the dashboard clock, at the same time noting Dunne's speed. It was very fast.

Bryce's hands rested on his knees and, seeing them, he was surprised to find them steady. They should have been as sweaty and shaking as poor Sammy Bean, spilling his story.

The story was, Sammy had been hired to take three passengers to La Havre where they were taking a freighter to—where? South America? Australia? Hong Kong? Sammy didn't know. The story was, the arrangements had been made by a man who kept a barely profitable farm this side of Dublin. A breeder of wolfhounds and

138

horses, who had used Sammy before for a spot of fishing and a bit of harmless smuggling of pups between Ireland and Britain. The story was, he had a daughter, a very pretty daughter who on her graduation from convent school some months back had made a trip to Boston to visit her American cousins. There she had met a charming older lad from her homeland. She came back a few weeks later not knowing she was carrying his child, but knowing full well he was not the blameless man he had first appeared to be. She was young, she was in love, but she might have gotten along without him had there not been this swelling of her belly. The story was, her father, when he was told was more than unhappy, he was scared shitless, beat her black and blue and uselessly forbade her to inform her lover of the coming baby. It was not an original story, what made it dramatic was the extremity of the personality involved. Because he loved her or because he had a sudden yen for fatherhood, or because he would take what was his and would not allow some farmer to decide what he should or should not have, whatever the reason Vox had cut a swath through Ireland, settling old scores. The story was, her Da had a change of mind and sent the girl to him and at Vox's request arranged the passage—possibly because none of his old associates wanted anything to do with him—out of the country. It might have worked, but there was a snag in the story. The snag being one of the girl's brothers. Digusted by his sister, by Vox, and perhaps by his father himself, he called McGarrity and gave him Sammy. She deserves whatever she gets, the little slut, he'd told Dunne incurring Dunne's everlasting disgust. She was his sister and whatever else a sister might be, to Dunne she was always family. But Sammy had one last twist on the tale.

"The story is, I've got a friend who has a cousin left of the law. This friend pilots a plane for hire out of Dublin airport. His cousin hired him to take a party of three out the same day I was hired, to the same destination. My friend was suspicious. There's been another plane hired last week in Limerick and the fare never

showed. Rumor was Vox had hired it then got sidetracked
and his lad had moved out of Shannon double-quick.
Knowing his cousin's weakness for talk under the influence of a bit of alcohol he took him home for a little
oiling. The story is, according to his cousin, Vox is going
by to see the father before leaving the country. Wants
to ask for the girl's hand like an old-fashioned suitor.
Wants to see the old man sweat, is the cousin's opinion,
wants to make sure the Da didn't set him up when he
hired me. So he hires my friend in Dublin to keep his
options open. And you never know with Vox, says the
cousin, he'd talked of going to Dublin. And the farm is
near the crossroads. He can go to Dublin or bypass it
altogether and go to the village where my boat is waiting.
But one thing's for sure, he's going to see the Da. Be
on my boat tomorrow night or take the airport," Sammy
had said, squeezing his hands together.

McGarrity had asked, "So will the girl be with him?"

Sammy didn't know. Sammy was spent; tired and sick
and dripping wet.

So the question was, as McGarrity had been quick to
point out when it was the three of them alone again, the
question was, would Vox risk taking this girl into a trap?
The question was, if it was Katharine on that plane to
London what was she doing going back to Dublin? The
question was, could Vox's girl have used the plane ticket,
the apartment, used Katharine's clothes, even her perfume?

Thinking ahead, Dunne brought Bryce back to the
present. "You'll be needing a place to stay tonight,
Kevin. My mum and and I would be glad to have you,
whatever happens."

"Thank you," Bryce said, then put more effort into
it, "thank you very much." He looked at the dashboard
clock again. "How much longer do you think it will
take?"

"We're almost there now, Kevin."

The question was, would they get there in time?

Five

Mick had left the shop in a sweat; upset for the money spent, for the high-handed treatment he'd received at the hands of the posh saleswoman, and for the itchy sense of pleasure and guilt looking at the scarf had given him. Yet it hadn't taken long, marching up the street with his Brown Thomas bag, before he was changing his attitude. He'd shown her, hadn't he? Made her get the scarf, paid for it without trouble, got exactly what he wanted. He snuck a look in the bag. God, it was a fine purchase, wasn't it? Maire'd know how nice it was, that he'd parted with plenty of money for it. Wouldn't this press on her his sincerity?

He approached his mail with such confidence that he wasn't surprised when he saw a letter with a Saudi Arabia return address. (He'd bought the scarf for luck, hadn't he?) Her stationery was the thin blue airmail kind but always touched with scent. Maybe she did it deliberately, or maybe the paper picked up the scent from cream on her hands or perfume at her wrist because the smell was so light you weren't sure if it was really there or if it was only your imagination, remembering. He tucked the Brown Thomas bag under his arm and tore open the envelope.

His sight was such that he had to hold the paper almost an arm's length away at an angle, and still had to squint. It was some time before he could decipher what that neat feminine script had to tell him.

He folded the letter carefully and put it inside his coat

141

pocket because he wanted to read it again, over and over. That's how he was going to spend his afternoon, his evening, maybe his next week. Going over the bloody thing until he understood exactly what this woman was saying, analyze the implications, read between the lines. He stepped back outside, heading toward the bus stop, shoulders straight, as he anticipated his day in the pub, once more using his umbrella as a walking stick.

He didn't notice he was walking in the rain.

Six

He had shuffled his options like a deck of cards, spread them out face down and soon he would have to choose. He glanced at the back seat where the girl lay under a red blanket. He could not see her face, only her tangle of dark curly hair, but her breathing was regular and quiet. She seemed restful. Unlike the driver. Brian was fast and cheerful and had trouble sitting still. He was a chatty lad when he drank but he hadn't had any problem staying off the drink when it became an order. He was too young to know he could die. Even the bang on the head from that motor accident hadn't slowed him down any. But Vox knew the risk was great. He had never doubted it was a kill-or-be-killed world. All his life, he had kept this fact in the forefront of his mind, never allowing himself the luxury of complacency, lest he forget the dangers that surrounded the everyday world. Every action he had taken was an effort to get his meanings clear, to express his thoughts perfectly. He had never underestimated the risk. If he had he would have been dead before now. He knew the longer he kept up this type of life, the more the odds were against him. And every day he beat those odds he felt the rush, something inside that said, *yes.*

The stakes now were the highest they had ever been. Yet he kept delaying his exit, tempting each victory with defeat. What did he want from her father? A blessing? Yes, he did. That was a determination he did not understand. I'll treat her well, he'd tell him. Set her up like a queen where we're going. A need for approval bound up with the need to look her father in the eye and judge a potential enemy. Some might see it a perversion of the convention, to ask for the hand of a pregnant bride and use it to test the father-in-law to be, but he needed to know whether to allow in the future the access to her family he felt sure she would one day request. She spoke of them too loyally; loyalty was deeply ingrained in her character. Her seeing her family might bring him danger, but it was one he might be able to calculate. It was danger from an unexpected source that would get him. For protection from that he had to depend on instinct, but his was sharp.

He would have fifteen minutes coming back from the farm. Fifteen minutes from the gate ahead to the crossroads to decide on one route or the other, on a last temptation. And what was he expecting from Nell? Another blessing? Was it the compulsion to show a new love off to an old? Or a signal to Nell that he meant to do one good deed? Take on a responsibility? Perhaps Nell would know. She always had been good at knowing things. She would understand this urge to complete all business, could interpret this dragging of his heels. The kind of life she had with Liam was a type beyond his imagination, but if he tried what was beyond his imagination—though not a life so poor—was that not risk too?

A few drops of rain fell heavily on the car windshield. On his right was a fenced pasture crisscrossed by a windbreak of trees. Two men were walking a pair of horses; one gave them no notice, the other looked at them with no more than casual curiosity. On the left roadside was another windbreak broken only by the gateposts of the drive they turned in. Soon after the gate the drive turned rough and the girl in the backseat groaned. A pasture lay before them, a cluster of horses at the far end gazing expectantly at the crop of farm buildings, an ancient coachhouse, a kennel, a modest white-washed house, and further on another stable. As they loomed nearer, the road grew rougher. He cracked open a window and listened.

"Carrie, my love," he called to the girl, "would today be a market day?"

Carrie, jarred by the road into semi-wakefulness, rolled on her back and answered sleepily, "I don't think so. No, it wouldn't be."

Vox put his hand on Brian's arm. The farm seemed quiet for a place with five healthy boys, helping its running.

"Slow it up a bit, lad," he told Brian. He put his hand under his seat and brought out a small machine gun for himself, he put a gun in Brian's lap. He kept looking at the buildings, wondering what clue might give the silence a reason. The buildings were arranged in an L-shape. The house faced the drive, the coachhouse and kennel centered alongside. Twenty-five feet later he knew what else was bothering him. The kennel had no dogs. He paused, having a moment when clarity hit him like a punch in the gut, then told Brian, "Back it up, lad. Back it up quick."

Seven

"*. . . said he thought* you might fall into a swoon. Silly fool, I told him, why did you not offer her a cup of tea? But Barry's shy with the ladies. My, but you're very pretty." The girl peered into Katharine's face. The girl's own complexion was clear as only really good fifteen-year-old skin can be, her features pretty with a practical set. She had what Katharine's own schoolday acquaintances would have termed *the kind of fat, fat boys like*. It was a phrase, in Katharine's memory, uttered with both derision and envy; mostly envy. She had greeted Katharine that afternoon at the B&B's door, determined to right all previous wrongs to hospitality. She must be the youngster who had knocked so firmly on Katharine's door that morning announcing breakfast. She had been ignored with equal firmness. Katharine finally got up at noon and left the quiet house without getting the promised meal. "I should have known. My brother's always so stupid with the pretty ones."

Flabbergasted, Katharine said, "It's kind of you to say so." Not kind to the brother, she thought, realizing her reply was quite out of kilter with the conversation. But the girl had no trouble following her disjointed train of thought.

"My mother before she died, God rest her, used to tell me, 'Don't run away from the sin of pride only to fall into the sin of hypocrisy.'"

Katharine couldn't help laughing. "A wise woman," she said.

"That she was. Not bad-looking either, for a mother. Dotty about crystal, mind you." It was a cheerful observation; a little defensive, as though to point out what might be considered a flaw before anyone else had the chance. Yet it was clear she was fond of it as it was; the excess of crystal being perhaps one of those eccentricities that made home *home*. They were in the front parlor where she had served Katharine tea and brown bread. She had lingered near the door, then slowly edged her way back, testing her welcome. "Anyway, I wanted you to have tea this afternoon. You didn't get your breakfast. I'm very sorry. I tried to wake you this morning."

"Yes, I know. I was visiting—" she started to say friends, but remembering Siobhan, she balked at the description "—and between that and the trip yesterday, I wanted to sleep in."

"Ah, yes, didn't get in until late, did you? Barry heard you come in—must have been two in the morning, he said. That's why I didn't knock harder. Thought you might need a lie-in. But, you see, I have to be at school at nine o'clock. I'd just as soon not go, but there it is, I have to, so there wasn't anybody to cook breakfast. We're mostly businessmen in the off season, or people for the horse sales, and they're always wanting an early start. I'm sorry you didn't get your breakfast."

"It didn't matter. I didn't want anything this morning." She hesitated, then asked, "Is it just you and your brother here?"

"Oh, no. My grandfather lives here too. Nearly deaf, though, so he stays downstairs and does repairs. Likes to read, too. History mostly. A lot of American history. God knows why, he's never been and he'll not go now, he's too old!" she stated with the cheerful brutality of the very young. "Likes the telly, too, but he has to play it loud. If it disturbs you up here, let us know. It's quiet this time of year—not many guests—so the sound carries. I've got two older brothers besides Barry. They're in and out a lot. In the summer they're here almost all the time."

Katharine sipped her tea. Had that been what she'd

heard the night before? Not fighting but television? She looked at the girl. She appeared quite happy about the arrangement of her life, to accept the responsibilities of running a B&B (for run it, Katharine was sure she did; there was an air of self-reliance and authority to her, despite her youth and prettiness) as a matter of course. Katharine wondered vaguely why the girl was standing there so anxious to chat with her. Perhaps she didn't get much of a chance to talk to anyone else. "I don't know your name," Katharine said.

"It's Dierdre," she answered, and grinned in a shy way, complimented and surprised at the suggestion she provide it.

"Pretty name. It's got a lot of history in the country."

"That's what the grandfather says. A lot of history, and none of it good. That's what he says about the whole country. Ah, well, you can't expect history to be nice."

"No. You'd be disappointed."

In agreement on this commonsense point there reigned an atmosphere of peaceful harmony. Katharine nibbled buttered bread. Briefly, a concern creased Dierdre's forehead.

"You weren't disappointed there wasn't a fire when you arrived, were you? We didn't think it was cold enough. We didn't realize you were an American. We don't get many Americans this time o' year. It's too cold."

"A fire would have been nice, but I'm used to the cold. I've been in Ireland for a while now." Katharine instantly regretted saying this and tried to steel herself against the barrage of personal questions she thought it would provoke.

But Dierdre's only response was: "And this is your first visit to Dublin, is it? Do you like the city?"

"It's lovely." True, even if her day had been disastrous. She'd wandered through the National Gallery, more interested in the decaying wallpaper than the portraits. The beautifully restored National Museum was hardly better. She kept thinking Kevin would enjoy the displays, kept catching herself reaching out to tug on his

sleeve. Again, she had been unable to make up her mind
on an eating establishment and had gone hungry. There
was no point in saying all this. "Really lovely," she
repeated. Dierdre was pleased.

"I can't imagine living anywhere else. Did you visit
the shops downtown? Brown Thomas is very nice."

"Yes, it is. I stopped in for a minute." She'd only
looked at the men's things. She did need a Christmas
present for James.

"You didn't find anything?" Dierdre managed to
sound both hopeful and resigned. Katharine shook her
head. "Ah, well, clothes come very dear, especially
there. There's a shop across the street that has some
lovely things—like the leather skirt you're wearing. Do
you find clothes expensive here? A lot of Americans do."

"It's been a while since I've been in America," Katharine answered. Diredre seemed to be asking for guidance rather than fishing for information or appraising her
income. Girl talk. It might have been comforting, but
Katharine had nothing to say. She hadn't so much as
glanced at the women's things and couldn't expect the
girl to be interested in the men's. Katharine did, however,
have the impulse to share. "I did find something at an
antique shop. Would you like to see it?"

Dierdre was enthusiastic. Katharine put aside her tea-
cup and they went upstairs. In her room, Katharine
showed Dierdre her purchase, the watercolor she'd seen
the night before in a shop window. She had wandered
around for over an hour trying to find it again. It was
very old and finely drawn. The long, delicately S-shaped
neck of the ostrich, the angle of the beak, even the tilt
of the feathered tail, articulated pride superbly. The military cap, so tiny on top of his head, the abundantly
decorated jacket, lent that touch of absurdity, while the
opium pipe suggested he was not so stable as he might
seem.

"Well, it's very unusual," Dierdre said, none too
quickly, and gave her back the watercolor. She clearly
thought the piece peculiar.

"Did you want more tea?" Dierdre asked brightly. "More brown bread?"

Katharine realized she'd been silent for some moments. "No," she said, "thank you. Can you tell me if there's a pub nearby where I can get a hot meal later?"

"Ah, Barry's the one that knows about the pubs. He doesn't go out himself much, but my older brothers talk to him. It would be easy enough to get a recommendation," she said, and happy to deal with practical questions rather than silence, she was gone.

Katharine propped the watercolor against the dresser mirror and sat on the bed. There was a bench at the foot of it covered in cream-colored velvet, and on it sat a fur felt hat Kevin had bought in a San Francisco travel shop not long before they'd left for Ireland. He'd been thinking of growing a beard, so there was two days growth on his face. She'd put that hat on his head as a joke and was surprised at the effect. It showed a side of him that was at once more playful and more dangerous. She'd talked him into buying it, but perhaps it was a side of himself he preferred not to advertise, or maybe it was just too theatrical for his nature, because he rarely wore it; kept it in the trunk of the car most of the time. He hadn't kept the beard, either. She hadn't been sorry. Having a beard had taken away the pleasure of watching him shave. She let out a long breath and picked up the hat. The inside smelled of the leather band there and on it was a reddish blond hair, more red than gold, with none of the gray evident at Kevin's temple. She plucked it from the rim and dropped it over the rug. She liked the hat, had brought it along with the rest of her luggage when she emptied the car. She wondered idly if security had gotten around to noticing the car and tracking its owner, if it was finally back in Kevin's possession.

Dierdre returned, her brother in tow. He told Katharine there were three pubs at the other end of the road. He named them, the last being ". . . an *excellent* pub. Serve a fine hot meal while the other two have but soup and sandwiches. I would have mentioned them last night, miss, but I thought you wanted a downtown restaurant."

"Will you be going out soon?" Dierdre asked. "In case you're out late again, what time will you be wanting breakfast tomorrow? School doesn't start until nine, and I don't mind being late." Katharine felt chastised· for having prevented the girl from doing her duty that morning. Still, she had no reason to get up early. Sensing her reluctance, Dierdre said, "I don't like school much, and they're used to my not being on time. Or I could leave a tray in your room tonight. A kettle and tea and cheese and brown bread, if you like. Or I could stay home, too." It took no second guessing to know what choice she favored.

"Oh, no, no. The tray sounds wonderful."

A bell rang downstairs.

"I'd better get the door; we've other guests tonight. I'll leave the tray, then," Dierdre said, disappointed.

She was off. Her brother stayed. Rather than shy, he gave the impression of being just soft-spoken, anxious to serve. "Being an American, do you prefer coffee?"

Katharine shook her head. He kept looking at her, though not in any way offensively. "Are you a Canadian-American? Your accent is different."

"No. I haven't spent much time in the States the last few years; that probably accounts for the accent. And the tea."

"My sister doesn't usually talk so much to guests. She wasn't bothering you, was she?"

"Goodness, no." The surprise was genuine and must have come through in her voice. He didn't seem to doubt her at all. He was, to all evidence, pleased, and smiled the gentle smile of a kind stranger.

"Well, then, you need anything, don't hesitate to ring the bell," he said, and left, closing the door quietly after him.

Katharine lay back on the bed and fingered the hat. Outside, the rain began to fall; fat, heavy drops that made a loud *splat!* against the old window glass. She put the hat over her face and tried to imagine a place of peace and repose.

Her imagination failed her.

Eight

The kennel had been a stable originally and each former paddock was completed by individual chain-fence runs. McGarrity would have liked to have left the dogs in their assigned places, but the problem of positioning men inside a paddock opening with four or five lanky fifty-pound pups all barking and jumping and shoving wet tongues in their faces proved impractical. The dogs had to be locked in the back stables. From time to time they could be heard howling. Two men had been assigned to each run and to every window of the old house. In the dead of night McGarrity had bussed in a veritable army. The bus was in the coach house. McGarrity had positioned himself behind the lace curtains of an upstairs window and surveyed the scene using a pair of field glasses. Shuttering through the windbreak of trees he could see a pale compact car making steady progress up the country lane. He spoke into a hand radio, "What do you think, lad?"

Dunne was stationed on the other side of the lane, to the far side of a horse. One hand held a radio in the pocket of his borrowed jacket, the other held a halter. He hung back as Bryce moved ahead, using Bryce as a kind of shield. He got a good look at the passing car, then pullled out the radio and said, "It's our man. We'll move."

Dunne replaced the radio and caught up to Bryce. Silently they let go of the halters and made a dash upward to the car hidden behind a windbreak.

* * *

"Two men in the front seat, Kevin, that's all I saw," Dunne told him.

Dunne was trusting him to drive, leaving his own hands free to work the rifle across his lap. Bryce was surprised, if relieved, to be allowed along. They didn't have to do this, they could have left him behind, they could have locked him up if they wanted to insure him out of the way. Dunne said, "Slow down. If we park across the gates he'll be blocked in. Not even Vox can go through that fucking line of trees."

Bryce let the car coast quietly a few inches more, for a better view. He could not see the men in the car sharply but, like Dunne, he could make out only two. He let out a deep breath. Vox's car was easing along very near the kennels. As long as Katharine was not in it they could shoot the hell out of it for all he cared. He put the gears in park, opened the door, began to take his protected place behind the car. Dunne made ready to follow. On Bryce's first step to the ground he heard Dunne say, "*Fuck . . .*"

As Bryce turned it was not the sudden reverse of Vox's car that struck Bryce cold, but the sudden rising from the backseat of a dark head. He didn't hear the first gunfire, only saw the car sink instantly down as the tires were shot. He saw the vehicle keep moving slowly, awkwardly, on flattened tires on a potholed road. He saw Vox display the aggressiveness he was famous for, saw him attempt the impossible. The door came open, Vox stood on the jam and began firing. Bryce saw what McGarrity wanted him to see, that they would be given no choice, that the resulting slaughter was Vox's decision, not theirs. There could be no complaints, not to the embassy, not to the press. Cruel method, but effective; consideration for a fellow officer in good standing.

"*NO!*" he thought he heard himself scream. But if he had the sound was drowned by gunfire as he stood helpless, having been placed too far from the action for the opportunity of even the dumbest heroics. He saw Vox stumble off the car, still firing. Moving on, littering the surroundings with his insides, turning bloodier, taking more bullets than anyone reasonably needed because of muscles that kept responding in their proscribed way long after life had given way.

He saw three years of memories wiped out in an instant, he saw in Vox's final moments a reflection of the rest of his years, bereft of life, motivated only by impulse. He felt himself shrink, dwarfed by the size of his loneliness and shamed by the inadequecy of his most practiced skills to prevent any of this. He was motionless, the pillar of salt. He felt a strong hand on his collar. He was crawling over the top of the car.

It had been a yellow car. It had been reduced to a piece of metallic honeycomb. Bryce didn't think there was a square inch without a bullet hole. He stood with McGarrity by the back door and he could see the girl, curled up in the corner, as though she had tried to make herself too small and inconspicuous for the bullets to find. But they had found her, several times over. She was a bloody mess, but she was not his bloody mess. Vox lay face down before them, the fine grey drizzle making a dark pudding of his blood and the surrounding mud. Dunne joined them, raising the hood of his jacket.

"He vowed never to be taken alive. I don't like to discourage a man from keeping his promises," observed McGarrity drily.

"He got very close to Dublin, didn't he," Bryce remarked.

"He might have been going straight to Drogheda."

"If that's what he was planning he was playing a mean trick on those people in Dublin. The woman thought he was coming. She'd been doing a lot of cooking and according to our check, buying double their usual rations," observed Dunne.

"Mean tricks were never beyond him," said McGarrity. He looked around, apparently satisfied, "Jesus, coming here was a stupid thing for him to do."

"Maybe you were right," said Bryce, "maybe this was a suicide run."

"Ah, well, we'll never know his intentions now." The

job being done, McGarrity had lost interest in the psychological tics of his quarry. He was only mildly speculative about one or two points of physical fact. "You notice the bloody young twit with him has a bandage on his head? I know of the lad, he's from Limerick. Wouldn't surprise me if he was the one who nicked your car, Mr. Bryce."

The wind came up and the rain began to fall thicker and heavier, as if to hurry the job of cleaning up. There was a lot of work to do and the men began doing it, despite the wet. McGarrity shouted instructions. Bryce looked at his watch.

"Is there a telephone inside?" Bryce asked.

"Sure there is," said McGarrity. "Go and use it if that's what's on your mind." Bryce started to move but McGarrity went on to remark, "If your woman went to London she must never have been with Vox at all. Damned perverse of the woman to take off and leave a car like that."

Bryce had nothing to say. McGarrity was obviously irritated by the red herrings that Katharine had thrown into his investigation.

McGarrity said, "Dunne will be leaving in an hour or so to make a statement to the press. He can take you with him. Unless you're in a hurry now, are you?"

"No," Bryce said quietly, "I'm in no hurry now."

Liam was sitting in a downtown fish and chips shop with his daughter Angela when the news came over the radio about Vox. The cook had the radio playing loud so everyone could hear, though what most of the youngsters in there were waiting for was the next song to be played. He would have thought that at the news he might have sighed relief or danced up and down, might even shed a tear or two. But he was too occupied with what Angela was telling him to react to the radio, and too preoccupied with what the radio was saying to react to Angela. He couldn't answer her, had no inclination to give advice, could not, in fact, separate one thought from another.

The only thing he could think to do was, on leaving Angela, spend the rest of his evening in the pub.

Nine

"*. . . Jesus Christ . . .*"

"No, no Christ here—"

"Not Christ, *Craig*. Katharine Craig."

"Eh?"

James sighed and started again. "My wife went to Dublin, but in the rush neglected to leave me the name of the place she was staying—"

"Neglected wife? My own daughter—"

"Is she staying?"

"—been dead now these three—"

"My wife—"

"You say we've talked before?"

"Yes."

"Speak up, lad!"

James was shouting already. "Yes, and we didn't get any further then, either!" He'd given up the first time, but now that he'd called everywhere else, this was his last hope. It was quickly going the way of all flesh. The keeper of the inn was either deaf, drunk, or eccentric, possibly all three. Bracing himself for a long haul, James leaned close to the table, opened a bottle of whiskey, and poured it into a glass.

"Having yourself a jot of whiskey, are ye?"

"*What?*"

"Ah, here she is. I'll hand her over directly."

"Katharine?" James said, surprised.

"My name's Dierdre. You're wanting to book a room?"

156

"I'm looking for my wife. Her name's Katharine Craig."

"Oh, sir, I'm hearing you fine. She's upstairs having a rest. Would you like me to get her for you?"

Having accustomed himself to incomprehension, and rather enjoying the opportunity to scream at the top of his lungs, this sudden switch to normalcy threw James for a minute. Did he want to give her a sporting chance to take off again, if she so desired? He delayed the decision, saying, "I'll be joining her this evening. Will that be a problem for you room-wise?"

"No, no trouble. But she said nothing to us about it."

"No. She doesn't know."

"You'll be surprising her then. Oh, that will be lovely."

"Do you think so?"

" 'Tis a sure thing, to my mind."

"She was rather upset at me a few days ago."

"She doesn't look mad now," she asserted confidently, "maybe a little depressed."

"Depressed?" He hesitated. "Would it be possible to order some flowers for her room?"

It was clearly not among their usual service, but it was also clear the girl approved. "You're very romantic."

"Yes," James said, "I am."

"And how much would you be wishing to spend?"

James thought for a moment. "Fifty pounds."

"Fifty pounds!"

She sounded very young, and James wondered if a woman of more mature years would greet his ideas with such cooperation. "I appreciate the trouble you're going to. Please pick up a small bouquet for yourself and add that to the bill."

"Oh, no, but you're very kind."

Imagining Kevin's face when he saw a fifty-pound surcharge for flowers on his room bill, he said, "We take our pleasure where we may. Don't tell her I'm coming. Let's leave it a surprise, shall we?"

After he hung up, James finished his whiskey. Having done his part to aid the two of them toward their happy ending, he considered his own plans. He ran his feet over the cold bare floor. He thought tomorrow he might go out and buy a rug.

Naw.

Ten

Mick wasn't drunk. By all rights, he should have been, but his body was wound up too tight, his emotions too full of injured pride and indignation, for alcohol to have had its usual effect. He kept picking up his drink, putting it down, hands roving from side to side, so the whiskey met its proper destination inconsistently. Liam, however, was having no trouble bringing the glass to his mouth, though he stuck to Guinness, which was not near so intoxicating as whiskey and good for you, according to the advertisements. If Liam kept up this pace, he was going to be very good indeed by the end of the evening.

His comfort to Mick came automatically, "She's a fine woman. But it is hard luck; no one's saying it isn't."

Mick stared moodily in Carmel's direction. It was another busy night. More of those handsome lads from the embassy were taking up space, and Carmel stopped at their table for a chat. She had a fine, firm figure, Carmel did, and a way of tilting her arse that was very satisfying to the viewer. Beyond them, Mick caught sight of Tommy coming up behind the new barmaid. They were in a dark corner near the entrance to the storage area where the extra condiments were kept. Mick had to strain to see Tommy slip his hand round the curve of the barmaid's rump.

That's the way to do it. Find yourself some nice bird. Do a man good, Mick thought. Tommy and the barmaid eased themselves firmly out of sight. Mick's hand found

the Brown Thomas bag containing the scarf he'd bought
that morning. After the bus had dropped him off near
Ballsbridge, he'd had an impulse to throw it in the canal,
ashamed of this physical testimony to his foolishness.
But he hadn't. And a good thing, too, it being such a
fine example of the perversity of women, the good faith
of men. He brushed a stray spot of foam off the bag and
pulled the scarf out carefully for display.

"Have a look, Liam. Have a look."

Liam handled it gingerly, admired it in a mechanical
way, this not being the first time he'd been offered the
scarf since he'd arrived. "Lovely. Any woman would
be proud to own such a thing. Here—" he waved his
hand to get Carmel's attention as she came around the
bar "—Carmel, what's your opinion?" he asked, de-
fering the responsibility of carrying on about it to her.

"'Tis lovely. Very fine," she said, matter-of-fact, and
started pulling pints from the tap.

"Put a hand to it, Carmel!" interjected Mick. "It's
wool and silk, the very best." He had showed it to Liam
in hopes Carmel would see, being interested in her re-
action. Carmel had said she'd been one of the ones to
hire the girl for Tommy, even helped make up the song
she sang; took a real interest in the joke between Tommy
and his wife, she must have. Sure. If anyone would see
the significance of the scarf, it would be Carmel. Mick
could imagine the little whips on it being a private joke
between the two of them. "I'd like knowing what you
think, as a member of the opposite sex," he added.

Carmel scraped the head off a Guinness with a knife,
then wiped her hand with a towel, less graciously than
she might have had she not been fetching pints for the
group of lads at the far table. She gave the scarf a quick
rub between three fingers. "Lovely," she repeated.

Mick was insistent. "And the pattern, Carmel? What
would you think of the *pattern*?"

"Lovely," she repeated more firmly.

"Now, Carmel," said Mick, who was hoping for more
enthusiasm or even a wink of the eye, "does it make

you think of anything in *par*-ticular? The pattern, I mean.''

''Ah, certainly,'' she said, rolling her eyes. ''Horse sweat and stable muck.''

''Carmel!''

This time she did wink before moving down the bar to deliver the Guinness.

Liam chuckled.

''The girl has no feelings!'' Mick remarked bitterly.

''She's just a young girl, Mick.'' Liam offered his sad comfort kindly. ''She's only got so much patience for the troubles of old men.''

Mick was greatly put out. ''You'd think she'd recognize quality when she sees it.''

''Ah, sure, maybe she does,'' Liam said, looking into his beer, ''maybe she does, but just doesn't care. She's young, after all. Don't know what you were expecting her to say.''

Drinking his whiskey, Mick glanced toward the storage entrance in time to see the barmaid walking out, adjusting herself along the way. It wasn't more than a minute or so before Tommy followed. Got his bit, Mick thought, and he wasn't any youngster. But then, neither was the barmaid. Mick shifted back to Liam, who was saying, ''My daughter Angela is going to be married.'' It was a proclamation issued without enthusiasm.

''Now, that's a fine thing!'' Mick looked surprised. So did Liam. The reply was full of good cheer, and the man Angela was marrying was nothing to be cheery about. Following Mick's eye to the door, Liam saw that a woman had entered the pub. Tall, wearing a leather skirt and a man's hat for protection from the rain, she headed straight for the bar. ''Look at that, will you, Liam. Got legs that would wrap clear around your neck.''

Liam never went in much for dirty talk or idle speculation of the sexual sort, and he was in no special mood for it now. But he thought it might be good for Mick, and even if it wasn't, he was used to accommodating him. ''Oh, sure,'' he said.

She conferred with the barmaid for a minute, then took a seat at a small table near the fire.

"A foreigner," decided Mick "French, do you think? Do we have a Frog here?"

Liam twisted around briefly to inspect her. He shook his head and returned to his beer. "American," he said.

"American," whispered Mick. "Do you think so? What makes you so sure?"

"There's an easiness to her. It's a quality Americans have."

"Ah, well," said Mick, "Americans have a loose way o' life—marrying and divorcing and such."

Liam frowned. "I only meant she can sit by herself and not look uncomfortable."

"Oh, sure," Mick agreed.

Mick wasn't really listening, and Liam hadn't the energy to explain any further. He ordered another pint and had it before him when he said, "Have you heard Vox is dead?"

"Is he now?" Mick said, interested.

"Got him late this afternoon, outside of Dublin."

"Well, now, good riddance," Mick said. "Jesus, it's been years since he was roaming the pubs here. Knew him, didn't you, Liam?"

Liam looked at him straight on. "So did you. I had to restrain you from becoming a bloody disciple once."

"Well, now, a good many of us ran into him from time to time. Sure. But there was no harm in it. Lot of life in the fellow, wasn't there? Hard to believe they got him. He did do the authorities a lot of damage. Still, I bet no woman ever gave him a bit o' trouble."

Liam stared at him. Mick sniffed and ordered a whiskey. For the next hour their conversation came in short bursts, as if to remind each other this was the reason they were here.

"Got a healthy appetite. Steak and kidney pie. Rice pudding. A pint. She's had herself a meal, hasn't she?" Mick had kept his eye on the American woman and noted her progress with satisfaction.

"Has she?" Liam wasn't interested.

"Do you suppose she's lonely?"

"If she is, she needn't be for long. When I went to the loo I saw the lads at the far table giving her the eye, though as far as I could see, she'd been ignoring them."

"A woman of taste, by Gawd" was Mick's fervent reply.

She was distancing her chair from the fire a little at a time. She hadn't brought a coat, but her sweater was thick wool, and her legs hosed with wool stockings. It had to be getting very warm where she was sitting, with the fire and so many bodies about, but other than moving her chair, she showed no signs of discomfort. In profile, she struck him as sad; being sad himself, he felt sympathetic. He made a loud sniff and finished his whiskey.

"Do you think she'd allow me to buy her a drink?" he asked Liam.

"You should be asking her, not me."

"Ah, well," Mick said, fixing his eyes away from Liam, "you know ladies always feel comfortable with you. I've come to believe it's because of your fatherly demeanor."

Liam slewed one eye his way. "Could be," he said. It was too bad, he thought, that Mick wasn't intending to tease. A good tease would have greatly improved his attitude. Ah, well, maybe Mick's deadly seriousness was a good joke in itself. And it was true enough, he supposed, that he was a father, and so, fatherly in his manner. He chuckled quietly.

"Sure now, Mick, if you want me to ask her so as not to cause yourself any embarrassment if she's not willing, I'll give it some thought." And before Mick could protest Liam's indelicate phrasing, Liam was quick to point out, "But if that's what you're wanting, you should speak up quick. She's heading this way, lad."

Eleven

Katharine was beginning to think the absence of Kevin Bryce in her life was akin to a peculiar vitamin deficiency, producing remarkable and seemingly unrelated symptoms. It was bad enough taking off for a meal into the rain leaving behind her leather jacket, but when that jacket contained her money, it was unsurpassed for sheer stupidity. Had this been the first incident of aberrant behavior, she might have been annoyed but not attacked by this sense of hopeless frustration, by the conviction any ordinary undertaking would be sabotaged by the part of her brain that flatly refused to function. In theory, leaving should be a simple matter of packing your bags and getting behind the wheel of a car; going from someplace uncomfortable to someplace comfortable. She had done it before, abandoning possessive friends, dubious business associates, and her most radical family member. This time it wasn't working. London, a city she loved, was a bleak landscape. The familiarity of James's flat had failed to dispense calm or comfort. She could not get from point A to point B without some dreadful error in judgment.

This mistake took the cake. Had this been her own village, there wasn't a pub that wouldn't have laughed and waved her on, knowing she'd be good for the money the next day. On the road, there is rarely a country kinder to travelers than Ireland, and in many villages she thought she'd been treated with more trust than any stranger deserves. But Dublin is a city, and cities anywhere are hard. To her own eyes, she appeared at best an idiot, at worst a vagrant, a potential con. Because she let the idea slip into her own mind, she thought a weakness might be perceived in her by others, the lack of confidence allowing them to put less stock in her honesty than they might have ordinarily. She would have liked to cry, but she was not one of those women whose tears inspire protectiveness in others. She was too big; size, like money, was more apt to inspire ridicule in times of trouble than sympathy. That was a lesson she'd learned early in life. There was nothing to do but square her shoulders and hope for luck.

At the bar, she explained her situation to a young barmaid who regarded her with an unfriendly eye and quickly turned her over to the owner himself. He was a pear-shaped man, soft belly and stout hips half again the size of his shoulders. His head, already proportioned too small, was made smaller still by features too large for it: lips and nose red and fleshy, a thatch of eyebrows black as if charcoal-sketched, protuberant blue eyes. He carried his ugliness like a mark of privilege.

"And how," he asked, stroking his chin, "do you propose to remedy the situation?"

"I was hoping—" *I was hoping you might offer a suggestion*, she started to say. But no matter how businesslike her delivery, there was something too virile, too earthy about this man—he reeked of opportunism. Two men a few seats down the bar were leaning into the conversation. She could imagine the hoots, the winks, and in this strange environment, her position was too vulnerable to accept them purely in fun. She removed her earrings. "—I was hoping you might hold these until I can go back to the house and get some money. They're very good pearls."

He looked at the earrings but didn't take them from her hand.

"Right around the corner apiece, did you say? Didn't think there was a B&B within blocks of here. I don't believe I've ever seen a sign."

"There isn't one," she said, and knew he was going to be difficult.

"Don't know anything about pearls. What would I do with them if you weren't to show?"

One of the two men spoke up, saying, "Give them to your wife. Tell her they're a present."

"For all the good it'll do you," said the other.

The owner gave them a quick, stern gaze, letting them know this too serious a business to be interrupted with lighthearted suggestions. He said to Katharine, "You haven't a credit card? I've never know an American without a credit card."

She sighed. "It's in the room, too."

"I see." He took the pearls but seemed patently uninterested in them, rolling them between his fingers, not granting a second's study. She kept her expression nononsense, but her face wasn't the part of her that held his attention.

"Or you could give 'em to your little bit on the side."

It wasn't said loudly, but the man swiveled his attention back to the two customers. "What was that, Mick?"

But Mick pursed his lips, and it was left to the other man to reply in a joking way, "Ah, well, your reputation as a ladies' man is well-known. Sure you could find some fine woman happy to take those pearls as a symbol of your chaste appreciation, Tommy."

His gaze lingered on the pair of them—one smiling, one sniffling and staring into his empty glass—before he said to Katharine, "You should be ashamed of yourself to have been so careless as to put us both in this uncomfortable position."

"I feel stupid, pissed off, but ashamed? Not bloody likely," she said. Somehow he'd been bested. She couldn't help smiling but kept the smile from getting too broad.

"Now you've been told, haven't you, Tommy!"

"Sure you have!"

"Give her back her pearls, Tommy. You can see she's no vagrant."

"Maybe," he said, chuckling. He was becoming such

a good sport, he had Katharine wondering if she'd only imagined the danger. "I will if you can give me, young lady, one good reason for doing such a stupid deed."

"A man," she answered, not missing a beat.

He slapped the pearls on the counter. "Good enough," he said, then seemed to reconsider, as if he'd been too easy. He pointed a finger at her. "But if—"

"If she doesn't bring it to you, Tommy, I'll stand good for it," said the heavier of the men.

Tommy laughed. "And that will be the last I see of you!"

"A small price to pay for such luck."

The unfriendly barmaid arrived back behind the bar in time to catch the last part of this exchange. She reached over and gently cuffed the big man on the shoulder. "You're a soft touch, Liam. Your daughters must put you through hell," She said.

"That they do, Carmel," he said, showing perhaps a slight lessening of his good spirits.

"Well, you needn't stand the debt alone. I'll put in half," said Mick.

"You won't have to stand the debt at all. Thank you very much, both of you. I do appreciate it. I'll run back to the room right now and get my wallet."

"No hurry, no hurry," said Liam. "It's cold and raining puddles, and you're wearing very little protection against such weather. My friend and I were just about to indulge in another round, and we'd be delighted if you'd join us."

She hesitated. The spontaneous offers of drink and conversation in this country was a custom Kevin had fallen into more easily than she had. But Ireland was disarming, and she had found that eventually she, too, could drift into unfamiliar company. She was never one to mistake curiosity for friendship; that had not changed. Yet Katharine was easier than she'd been three years before. Living with Kevin had softened her; the unconscious acknowledgment of being protected, having a place of refuge, automatically being accorded the respect of a woman with her own man, was with her even when he was not around, without her being aware of the change. What she told herself was: that she could look at the big man and know instantly he was kind, and the fact that this haughty barmaid should tease him so deferentially made her feel better.

"No harm in waiting to see if the weather will show you a bit o' kindness."

Perhaps, too, it would be ungrateful and impolite to refuse.

"A hot whiskey, then. Thank you."

She relaxed, sure she had done the right thing.

Twelve

"We've been admiring your hat."

It was resting on a fine, healthy head of hair they wouldn't have been able to see had she worn a scarf wound tight around her head the way most ladies did, hiding it all away. No, this was daring, more daring than a bare head, like one of those free-spirited girls in a posh magazine. Mick could state with perfect sincerity that he approved. But she responded to his compliment by taking the hat from her head and setting it on the counter. She combed out her hair with her fingers.

"Not proper protection, though, is it?"

She smiled and shrugged. "Listen, *thanks—*"

Liam said, "Never mind. Tommy's all right but inclined to push his weight around, like most of us, now and then."

"Bloody fool," Mick was obliged to add with feeling.

Liam sipped Guinness. Katharine punched the clove-studded lemon slice in her whiskey with a finger. So ended another spurt of talk. Introductions had already been made, the usual courtesies exchanged. Mick adjusted his tie, one eye on the back mirror. Classy-looking bird. What was it she said she did? Worked mainly making clay sculptures. Odd thing for a woman to do. Somewhere in his mind he adjusted this image to modeling pottery jugs like he'd seen in the Kilkenny shop. Lovely, they were. Pretty and practical. He stole a look at her. She sat very straight; yes, very classy. Impossible to imagine her mucked up with clay. Should be taken care of, be provided for in a proper manner. Beyond his means, certainly. But then, he didn't want her for keeps. Just a bit of shared sympathy, that's all he was asking. Something to take the edge off of loneliness. Big, healthy girl on her own must be feeling it too. *A man*, she had said when Tommy asked her the reason for her empty-headedness. Been thrown over, most likely. Hard luck. But he'd been nice, hadn't he? And Liam. They'd been heroes, of sorts. Gotten her out of a jam, because there was no telling about Tommy, was there? He wished Liam would get on with the conversation. Liam never let him down, but he was broody tonight. Inconsiderate of him to be that way just when he needed him most. Bloody bad luck.

Liam might have had an inkling into Mick's feelings, if he'd given them any thought. But Liam's mind was not on the mood of his companion but on troubles of his own. The lady sitting next to him was stirring the thoughts already centered on his daughter Angela, making him think of her in a different way. Strange, he thought, because they didn't look anything alike. This woman was an amazon in comparison to his Angela, who was small and round, with a face as harmless as pudding (excepting, of course, when her temper was up). There was an edge to this woman's face; it was used to keeping secrets. He couldn't imagine Angela walking with the straight-back arrogance she did. And why couldn't he seem to use her name, even to himself? A presumption, he decided; it feels too familiar. Liam was an easygoing man, not one to often feel left out or to resent it when he was; he was surprised he felt so now. He didn't think he liked this woman, sensing in her heart there might be a piece of flint. But now he knew why he thought of Angela. The woman's face wasn't bland like most American visitors—it had character. Angela had character, though it had not yet been etched so firmly on her face. Marriage would take care of that, he concluded grimly.

Katharine sucked the sour taint of lemon off the tip of her finger. In the mirror she saw the three of them propped up at the bar against a backdrop of bodies swilling beer under pseudo-Tudor beams. The building was genuinely old, the decor wasn't. In the last 150 years, concessions to the current modernity had been made and replaced, made and replaced again, and Katharine found the attempt to go back further than its original era for the sake of tourism halfhearted and wholly unsuccessful. She didn't suppose the regular drinkers gave it much thought. She was obviously sitting next to two of them. Mick had lovely silver hair, but without his whispered words to Tommy, she probably would not have noticed him. Liam, on the other hand, had the rheumy eyes of a friendly but unhappy hound. Overweight, he would appear ill at ease in his suits from the first moment of dressing. He was sweaty and red, and his hair circled a bald spot like a wreath of laurels. His mouth was full and shaped as if used to smiling, a perfect balance for those eyes. He wasn't smiling now, and Katharine was all too aware that these two men were cronies, used to a steady stream of talk. She found herself uncomfortable with the continuing silence. She didn't want to impose on them, and in the sweet distance of small talk, she hoped for peace herself.

"Been shopping?" she asked, seeing a Brown Thomas bag.

Mick's first inclination was to snatch the bag away, banish the question. But Liam interceded.

"Give her a look, Mick." He said to Katharine, "Mick went out and bought a present for a friend—a lady—and he's been anxious to get a woman's opinion on his purchase. Perhaps you'd be so kind as to let us know what you think."

Mick fumbled with the bag. It was losing its crispness; overuse had made it soft at edges smudged with finger marks and beer blots; the tissue had been opened and closed without regard for its original folds. The scarf tumbled out into Katharine's hands, an untidy mass she handled gently.

"The fabric feels wonderful. Wool and silk, isn't it?"

"There now, Mick! And what do you think of the pattern? Is it suitable?"

Katharine smoothed it out across her lap. The pattern seemed conventional enough to her. Not something she would have picked for her own, but nice.

"What sort of woman is she? What does she like to wear?"

Mick pursed his thin lips in thought. There was a swift, almost imperceptible, flare of his nostrils before he began, answering the second question rather than the first. "Well, she dresses conservatively—simple skirts and blouses, plain jumpers. But always good ones," he was quick to point out. "Appreciates quality, she does. Never any loud colors. Good tweeds; even has one cashmere jumper for good. She's one of those women who always has the best of everything. You know the kind I mean?"

"Yes."

Mick was warming to his subject. "But not extravagant. If anything, a little on the mean side. Buys quality because it lasts." He sniffed. "She's younger than me, young enough to have children, if she liked. But conservative. Always got her eye on the future."

"I'm sure she'll love this, then," she said, folding the scarf and setting it on the bar.

"Ah, well, she's never going to see it, is she?" He couldn't hide the bitterness.

"Ah, now, Mick," said Liam, "don't be that way."

"It isn't me. It's her."

Afraid of another awkward silence, Katharine adopted the directness she had found so uncomfortable when she'd first come to Ireland. "You've had an argument?"

"You can't argue when there's thousands of miles between you, you can only shake your fist at the air." Mick put the whiskey to his mouth and drank.

"His friend is working for a company in Saudi Arabia," Liam explained. "We thought she was going to be home for the Christmas season, but a letter arrived today saying she'd be home for an extended stay in March and wouldn't be here for the holidays after all. Mick was disappointed."

"But you could send it to her, couldn't you? It probably has time to arrive before Christmas."

"That isn't the point. The point is, saving a few hundred quid was more important than being with me. She's got the money. *I've* got the money, I could buy her the ticket. She even wrote that in her letter—that she knew I'd pay if she asked. But she thought it was a waste since she was coming home so soon. So soon! It's three bloody months!"

"Yes, that would be disappointing," she said, more sadly than she realized.

Mick found her sympathy encouraging. He went on to say, "I'd be there in an instant if she wanted me, the cost be damned. If you love someone, you want to be with them. It's only reasonable."

"Didn't realize you were such a romantic," Liam commented dryly.

Mick shot him a sharp look.

"It sounds reasonable on the surface," Katharine said.

"It sounds reasonable! It is reasonable! Simple as two and two."

"I don't think anything's ever that simple," she said.

"Of course 'tis. Why wouldn't it be?" Mick's face was set like the wizened, bawling baby in the pram. The passion wasn't so surprising; raised voices and vehement language took place every evening in the pub.

"Because we come into love with too much excess baggage," she said.

Mick blinked. Liam regarded her more attentively over his pint.

"I mean . . . I suppose if you were bonded at birth, it might be easier for two to become one, so to speak." She smiled bleakly. "As it is, you've had time to develop things about you that are different—experiences, needs, suspicions—than the one you care for. And in doing so . . . well, it causes misunderstanding as you discover just what or who you've decided to live with. If, in fact, you have decided to live together. If it's actually possible for you to live with that particular person." Used to Kevin's level of precision, she realized her speech was not well organized. She took a long swig of whiskey.

"Well," said Mick, "that's what I was saying, wasn't it? You stick together. You work it out."

Katharine frowned.

"You wouldn't put off the man you loved just to save a few quid, would you?"

"No . . . but that doesn't mean I might not do something else. Your friend, where does she come from? What's her background?"

Liam spoke up as though to forestall any storytelling, any glossing over of the facts. "Maire comes from Limerick, from a family of fourteen. It was a rough neighborhood and very poor circumstances."

Katharine nodded, not feeling the need to elaborate on the self-evident.

"She doesn't need to worry for the future, if that's what you're thinking," Mick said. "I've told her I'd provide for her. I've given her my word."

Katharine raised an eyebrow. She phrased her answer carefully.

"I'm sure she knows you're an honorable man, that you'd always do your best. But if she's used to fending for herself, she probably feels more comfortable not putting you in that position."

Liam's mouth twitched.

"But I want to provide for her. I want her to know she can depend on me. She's a smart girl, all right. She can make her way. But I've got to be good for something. I've got to be of some use to her. Otherwise, why should she put up with me?"

Katharine flinched. She used to pay Kevin half the rent until she discovered he banked it back into her account. If they were at the grocery together, and they usually were, because he liked to cook and was better at it than she, he always paid. Denied the role of accomplished provider in her life, were these overtures a throwback to an idea as old as there were men and women? If she bought drinks at the pub or dinner at a restaurant, he never argued; he rarely bought her presents any time other than the traditional occasions. She felt her stomach knot. Yet Kevin had bought a houseful of furniture, most of which was to her liking.

"Ah, Mick," said Liam, "don't be thick. How many times have promises been made only to be broken later? It's nice to hear, sure. But why would anyone want to bank their future on it?"

Mick looked at him as if he were a traitor. "What are you saying, Liam? Are you saying my word's no good?"

"You know I'd never say anything of the kind. I'm only saying a woman has to look out for herself. Life is full of all sorts of unforeseen circumstances." He said to Katharine, "My wife, Nell, is illiterate. A smart woman. In fact, if you asked, that's what she'd say. I'm illiterate, not I can't read or write. She has a nice way of speaking. When we were young, I didn't encourage her to learn. I liked the feeling it gave me to read to her. I liked the feeling of being her teacher, of having her depend on me. She was so young and pretty, I just . . . but now she's afraid. She's no longer young, and it's not easy for her to learn. Didn't seems so necessary thirty years ago, but the world's getting more complicated all the time."

"But she's got you and the children," Mick said.

"And I could get hit by a bus on the way home from the pub, or knocked down by some of those bloody young twits on O'Connell Street, and that would be the end of me. Then what would happen to her? We've two daughters in America, a daughter in Australia, and a son that's no bloody use to man or beast. Nell wouldn't fancy leaving Dublin. Here, there's Angela . . . but as I was saying, sometimes there's circumstances that can't be known about or planned for."

Mick's eye fell on Katharine's empty glass. "Carmel," he said, flagging her down, "we're all in need of a refresher."

Katharine made a motion, about to object, when Liam suddenly made up his mind to pursue the opportunity Katharine presented. He could, he thought, be as pig-headed as Mick. It was not his nature to consult other people with his problems, or to spend time airing his grievances, articulating the faults of his friends and family. It was not his intention to do so now. But Liam did need to talk, needed to know if his daughter was an area beyond his expertise.

"You say you work doing sculptures. Do you make a living from it? Does it keep you well?"

"Yes. I'm one of the lucky ones."

"Ah, luck. We all need a bit of it sometimes. But it wasn't all luck, was it? You had to work hard."

"Yes."

"You would have to have been very disciplined for such a young age."

"I always felt compelled to do artwork, but when I turned eighteen, I applied myself to it exclusively. I had no distractions. At the time, there was nothing else for me but work."

"Nothing but work!" Mick was incredulous. "So young. A pretty girl—in California, didn't you say earlier? Where there's sunshine and beaches and water sports like—what was it we saw on the telly here last week—*windsurfing*? You've got to have been enjoying yourself." Mick conveyed his disbelief indulgently, as though she didn't mean to be dishonest but just wasn't in full possession of the facts. Both Katharine and Liam ignored him.

"You've done some traveling? Seen the world in the course of your work?"

"Some of it, yes."

Liam examined her thoughtfully. "And not all of it good."

"Ah, well," said Mick, "any country is easy when you have money."

Liam turned on him and made no attempt to hide his impatience.

"Mick, the sum total of hard circumstances doesn't revolve around money."

"Money's more important than me, that's all I can see," Mick said, offended.

"You don't see because you refuse to."

Spurred on by a need as urgent as Liam's, Katharine

was not about to allow him to be sidetracked into an argument with Mick. She tapped him lightly on the hand.

"You're asking me for a reason?"

Liam focused back on her, forgetting Mick entirely.

"You have a husband?"

"No."

"But you have a lover?"

"Yes."

"And you love him?"

She didn't hesitate. "Yes."

Their fresh drinks arrived. Mick's new whiskey went down easy. Liam's old pint stayed where it was, unfinished.

"But he gets in the way sometimes, doesn't he?"

"Yes."

"And your family, did they get in the way?"

"Most of them had died by the time I was thirteen. When I was of age, I left the cousin who was my guardian. I didn't love him."

"Just like that, you walked away."

Equally speedy, equally anxious, she said, "I had to."

"And your lover. He doesn't work an ordinary job, does he?"

"No, he never has."

"Are you happy with him?"

She stalled. Liam didn't let up, demanding she respond, advancing further.

"Have you changed his life?"

"I didn't mean to, but yes. He left a job that was important to him to be with me. It's the way I work. I can't seem to stay in one place. Everything's different for him."

"Are you happy with your work?"

"Are you happy at Guinness?"

"It puts bread on my table."

"It's no different for me in one sense. In another, it's like air. You don't worry until it's not there anymore."

"So you can't give it up?"

"Could you give up Guinness?"

"Not without starving."

"Same with me."

"We're not talking about the same kind of starvation, are we?"

"We are and we aren't."

"You're playing with me." Liam sat back and, in that small action, managed to incorporate both dignity and hostility.

His pulling back made her want to continue all the more. "You're playing with me. You're picking my brains without clueing me in to the purpose of the questions or the consequences of my answers."

Liam leaned close enough for her to appreciate the quality of his bloodshot eyes: the intelligence behind them, the strength of spirit that gave them life. "And that scares you, love?"

"Shitless," she said and meant it.

"But you're going along with it. *Why?*"

"Maybe because I need the practice."

"But it's nothing unless you're risking something. Nothing but cheap thrills. Because that's the way your sort is. You'd rather be scared to death than bored to death," he hissed.

"Even I have things I'm afraid to put at risk."

"Ah, but you're going to have to risk them. Otherwise you're bullshit."

Katharine sat completely still. Mick's mouth dropped open, and into it entered whiskey. He quickly signaled for another.

"My daughter Angela is marrying someone like you, and I don't think I like it."

Mick, anxious to retrieve a position in a conversation that had lost him, said, "Angela's a grand girl, Liam. She'll be fine."

Liam spoke sharply. "If you had a daughter of your own, then maybe you'd understand, Mick. You don't want to see them stuck with some layabout."

"Well, it's not my fault I haven't got any, is it?" Mick slid off his bar stool and made his way unsteadily to the loo.

Liam said to Katharine, "I don't believe this man's a

layabout. Sometimes I think I'd like it better if he was, because I see in him what I've seen before. I saw it in a man who stayed with us once, I see it in you, I see it in myself. I've done damage in my time. I was a leader not always wise in my leadership. I took Nell from her home in Belfast, I tried to show her a freer way o' life. I wanted her to live, really live, fully. I wanted her to sing and dance and be open to experience. I didn't take into account that perhaps she didn't want such freedom. That it was not only freer than Ireland would allow, but freer than her own heart could take. She tried to follow my steps at great cost to herself. It might be that I would have been better off teaching her to read. I was selfish in my lessons, and I've been living with the effect ever since.''

She didn't attempt a consoling response; she waited for him to continue. He spoke very low and persuasively.

''Angela does paintings. That's where she met her young man, in one of these classes she takes. She'll have a lot to keep up with, marrying someone like him. I don't want to see her worn down. When you get married, people expect certain things out of you. And I'm not sure Angela's got what it takes not to fall into it all. She'll find out soon enough it's the woman who's expected to do all the giving. And he's one young man who won't respect a doormat, even if he asked for one. If she doesn't stand up to him, I think he could be a bastard.''

He paused, holding back. Katharine said, ''On the other hand—?''

''On the other hand, if she stays on her own, manages some success so life isn't cold studios, cast-off clothes, and dry bread for meals—I know how it is, I've had friends in all walks o' life—in another ten years time, is she going to be like you? I'm not sure I'm fond of that idea, either. Goddamn all independent, aren't you?'' The conclusion was made just respectfully enough not to be flirtatious, just angry enough to avoid being patronizing.

"When you look at your daughter's work, does it make sense to you?" she asked.

"Can't make head nor tail of 'em."

Katharine pushed harder. "Can't you?"

Their eyes held fast.

"Calling my bluff, are you? Maybe I can. That's what art does if it's good, isn't it? Makes you think. Has an effect."

"Supposedly."

"If it's true, if it's honest, it's unrealistic to think it won't. It's what your own things do, isn't it?"

"I don't see the effect," she said.

"You leave your mark without having to deal with what you leave behind, is that what you're saying?" There was a perception, a thrust, in the tone of his voice that made her flush to the roots. "Is that what's troubling you? You told Tommy a man was the reason for your bit o' carelessness. You say you've had an effect on your lover. Do you not like your own handiwork?"

She shook her head, partly a denial, partly trying to keep down what she'd been suppressing for some time. But it was time, time to speak of what she feared, whether she liked it or not.

"He's been buying a lot of things—household things, I mean. I've always believed spending money was what people who were unhappy did. In my experience, watching my guardian particularly, it was what you did to make up for all the emotional things you didn't have or couldn't give. I see all those things and I feel ashamed. I don't *trust* them."

"You think you've made him unhappy. You think he's sorry that his life is changed and he can't change it back. Join the land o' the living, my love. And what about yourself? Are you sorry? Do you regret it all?"

"No." Her answer came out so strong, she surprised herself. Liam wasn't shocked at all. The corner of his mouth turned up. "But if he leaves, I don't know how I'll piece myself back together again."

"'Tis a very strange comment coming from a woman who's probably already done the leaving herself." For the first time, she tried to avoid his eye, but he wouldn't let her. He touched her chin with the rim of his pint glass and eased her around.

She said, "And fucked it all up. You wouldn't believe the stupid things I've done in the last week."

" 'Tis a strange woman who doesn't appreciate a bit o' comfort—a home. Have you not told him how you feel about your life with him?"

"As I've been sitting here tonight, I've wondered if maybe he doesn't actually like all that stuff, doesn't maybe need it. He told me he needed it and I never believed him. Now, if I ask him to get rid of it, won't I be demanding he change again? How much can I change—how much can he change, without one, or both of us breaking?" She did not expect an answer.

Liam gave a shout of laughter. It was a deep and unquestionably attractive sound, as young as Kevin's, who had to be twenty years his junior. "You don't know how much better this makes me feel. Maybe there's still aspects of this world that aren't completely beyond my understanding. If there's one thing consistent, it seems people will love and be stupid. Here I thought I was being progressive with my daughters—especially the youngest—and I find I'm like the rest of Ireland, being pulled into the twentieth century, kicking and screaming, while the rest of the world moves into the twenty-first. And being a hypocrite to boot. There's a part of me that regrets not a thing with my Nell. I love her, and the selfish part of me says—she's here, she's close, we fight, we've hurt, but we've loved. Yet I'd like to deny my daughter her chance with this young man because I can't look at him and know he'll need my daughter. I look at her paintings and I'm surprised at them. She's only twenty; there's a lot of things I don't know about her, much less her love."

Katharine suggested hesitantly, "You want the best for the people you love, but you don't actually know what they need or if it's your job to provide it. That's a problem you find in any country."

"Are you telling me I'm conceited, Katharine? Thinking I'm the only one with difficulties?"

He was teasing her. It felt as intimate as if he'd touched her, something she knew he would not do. Recognizing the sense of regret, she smiled slowly and shook her head.

"Well, maybe you should. You're seeing a side of me only my wife is after seeing."

"What side is that?"

"The shitty one."

"I've missed seeing the shitty side of an intelligent man," she said ruefully.

He studied her with a sensitivity she had also missed.

"So you think me intelligent. It must be true; I don't think you're that kind of tease." He swirled the last inch of Guinness around in his glass before he spoke again. "I was thirty years old when I got married, and I've been married for thirty years—were you even born when I took the vows?"

"Depends on what month you were married," she said.

They both paused, savoring an exchange that had no practical place left to go. Liam said, "We're a mess, aren't we?"

There was a certain camaraderie in that. She lightly clinked her whiskey glass against his pint. There was no telling which of them started laughing first. But it was obvious to anyone who cared to pay attention that they had made great progress in their acquaintance.

Mick stood at the fringes of the crowd, watching them laugh.

Thirteen

"Have you heard of the man called Vox? He's died this very day, outside o' Dublin. Used to be quite the lad about town many years ago. Had my share o' drinks with him then. He'd been giving the authorities no end o' trouble recently."

Mick's reentry into the conversation was one of those moments that made Liam wonder how they'd ever been friends. Sure, it started with sympathy after Mick's wife ran off with Nell's brother. But they hadn't seen each other regular until after Mick had been in the hospital the year before. It was sad to see a man having so few visitors. He wondered what Maire saw in him. He knew her to be a plain woman without too much imagination, a hard worker possessing a good disposition and a sense of humor. Maire appreciated in Mick his generosity, his consideration, the fact he never hit her. That must count for plenty.

"He's been a terrible criminal. Still, he's lived his life beholding to no one, laying himself down for no man. You've got to admire him for that, is my thinking."

Liam said, "I am no longer young. My admiration is not wooed so easily."

"Well!"

Thick as a brick and probably shitfaced too, before long. Maire being in Saudi Arabia seemed to be rotting away the last of Mick's pleasant qualities. He was afraid any continued conversation along these lines would aggravate an inclination in himself to thrap Mick, and there was no use thrapping Mick, because he was Mick and not somebody reasonable. He was more afraid it might rob him of the feeling of renewal the last few moments had given him. He wanted to go home and make love to Nell. He turned abruptly to Katharine.

"It's time I should be making my way home. Would you humor a man of my generation this once? Let me put into practice a bit o' chivalry. Allow me to buy your dinner."

In an appropriate mixture of sincerity and humor, she bowed her head, saying, "I would be honored."

Mick made no objections to his leaving.

"Go on, have another. For the road. I've already stood the round."

He'd ordered it when she went to the loo. They'd get along fine, he was sure, now that Liam wasn't there to detour the conversation his way. The woman needed sympathy, not bullying the way Liam had done. And Mick was prepared to be sympathetic, by God. He inched the whiskey closer.

Katharine hesitated. During the few months she had lived with Kevin while he was a cop, there was one phrase she'd heard often enough at the station for it to make a lasting impression. *What goes around comes around.* Hardly original and not particularly profound, she supposed. Perhaps she had been most impressed by its multiple uses—a joke, a threat, a justification, an explanation, an epitaph, a philosophy of life, the conclusion of many an anecdote, and once, a benediction. The idea fit her own superstitions, fit her tricky do-unto-others philosophy that required a common sense not commonly found. She sat down.

Nursed on whiskey, the grievance against the distant Maire grew fat and energetic.

"—been married more than twenty years—did I tell you? But only lived as husband and wife for two before she took off to America with a bloody salesman from Belfast. I'm told the woman's alive and doing well, living in Boston. So I'm stuck. I can't get married, I can't have

a family. Didn't bother me so much until I met Maire.''
He shook his head, a vague, hopeless gesture, as though
after twenty years the enormity of his loss had just
dawned on him. ''Maire won't have a child without the
benefit of the Church.''

''Does she want a child?''

''O' course she does.''

''Has she said so?'' Katharine asked, carefully.

Mick jut out his chin. ''Well, she doesn't talk about
it much. But she's always smiling at the children when
we go to the park. She's good with them, she is.'' He
paused, and the expression on his face held both doubt
and fear beneath the anger. ''I asked her once, if someone
younger and free should ask her to marry him, what
would she say? You know what she answered? She didn't
know. Now, what do you think of a woman like that?''

Katharine couldn't help wondering how he'd put the
question to her. ''Has she said she loves you?''

The question clearly shocked him. ''O' course she
has!''

''Well, from everything you've said, she sounds like
a straightforward, sensible woman. If she says she loves
you, she probably does. If she says she doesn't know if
she'd marry someone else, she probably doesn't. I'd
guess she thinks too much of you to lead you on, make
you a promise she's not sure she can keep. That doesn't
mean she will marry someone else. It's like asking what
you'd do if you were on a ship that was sinking—you
won't really know until it happens. You're lucky to have
someone honest and outspoken.'' Her attention drifted
away from him, so in his next question, she missed the
subtle alteration of his tone.

''What would your lover be like, now? Would every
woman look at him should he walk into this pub this
very night? Is he a handsome lad?''

''Yes,'' she answered, too quickly, and caught herself.
Was he handsome? He was over forty and looked it. He
was solid and thick in the middle. He was red-haired and
freckled, though, thank God, his skin had enough pig-
ment in it to keep him from looking the perpetual measle

victim. His nose was snubbed. His hands were sturdy, working-class hands. She had forgotten he wasn't the first man you noticed when you walked into a room. She smiled and shook her head in amazement.

Mick pinched his nose between his fingers and tugged at it roughly, sucking in air as he released; a disgusting gesture for a disgusting thought.

"Sure, I think I know just the sort of young fellow he is." He did, surely. Tall and sun-blessed. "What would he think of your sitting here in the bar this evening?"

She hadn't heard him. "Pardon me?"

He raised his voice.

"I said, what would he think of your sitting alone in the bar having a drink like this?"

She frowned. "I don't suppose he'd give it much thought."

O' course he wouldn't. Free and easy, these Americans, like Liam said. Her hat was sitting on the bar. He couldn't help staring at it. Carmel was announcing the last call for drinks. He said to Katharine, "One more."

"No. Thank you."

She was, to Mick's growing irritation, unshakably sober. Any normal woman would be feeling a little high.

"I have a place downtown. Perhaps you'd like a drink there? Where it's quiet."

Her eyebrow shot up. He would have liked to slap it back down again, shut her whole bloody eye with the back of his hand.

"Ah . . . no. I'm afraid not."

He leaned closer.

"But what were you thinking of, sitting there? Did you not expect the evening to end in some kind of excitement?" At the word *excitement*, his face trembled as if he had one of his own he could hardly contain. She turned away. He looked and saw the boys from the embassy. "Ah sure, you don't mind a bit o' company. Is it that you fancy someone younger? Have you got your eye on one of the lads over there? I'm only wanting to know. No hard feelings, is there? Just trying to understand. It means nothing to me."

From one moment to the next, his eyes had grown alarmingly red, and his face blotchy from drink.

"It's time I should be going. Thank you for the drink."

Taking the hat in hand, she stood, towering over him tall as Lady Liberty. His cheeks were tingling. The surrounding background was increasingly fuzzy, but he saw Katharine silhouetted clearly against it. What he noted most was the way she dropped the hat on her head. She took it by the crown, adjusting the fit, back to front, like a man. "And this work of yours, where has it got you?" Her clear gray eyes regarded him peacefully. He would have preferred some anger. He would have preferred a shouting match. What sort of woman was this to cause such a rift between himself and Liam? He wanted to rip that bloody hat off her head. "Can't be doing you any good at all. Bumming drinks and dinner off old men. Is that your racket? Why, *anyone* would think you're an easy piece. But no, you're choosy. What is it, am I not man enough for you?"

It was the way she looked at him, then that gentlemanly tug at the brim of the hat, that brought Mick up off the stool. *Bloody cheek!* He blinked and the crowd parted and closed in around her like water. For he was sure it had been no longer than the blink of an eye before he was up. Moving quickly, wasn't he? Everyone was tilting out of his way; noisy as hell, a regular roar in his ears, cheering him on . . .

Fourteen

The rain was a soft, swirling mist under the streetlamps, dense enough to keep the light an orange bulb dangling close below the iron. She stepped off a curb into a gutterful of water, soaking herself to the ankle, and crossed the intersection to make her way up the avenue of brick houses and white doorways. This was a well-bred neighborhood, and while lights were on in many of the houses, there were no curtains drawn to give any clue to the activities inside. She would have liked to see people carrying out the normal rituals of a November evening. Breathing deeply, she tried to exorcise the smell of too many bodies in too small an area, too much smoke, too much whiskey over stale breath. All that waited for her was a big yellow room that had nothing in it that was a part of her except a suitcase of clothes, so she didn't hurry. Sighing, she stopped to look at the street behind her. A couple of cars drove by, blinding her with their headlamps. Her legs ached, they always did when she was overtired, and the wet foot didn't help any. She turned slowly up the street, using the undignified gait of one solid step, one squish. *He could have found me if he wanted*. Childish. Unfair. Until tonight, she would have been furious if Kevin had. She rubbed her nose using the back of her sleeve. The world was unkind and Kevin was a vastly superior man. No great revelation. If she could only learn how to balance this delicate business of living with someone else, for she did want to live with someone, dammit. Very much.

A heavy glop of wet smacked the side of her neck and slid a jagged snake's crawl down her back. Disgusted, she looked at the tree branch above her and caught a flash of movement from behind. A distant figure was hurrying up the street.

You've got to take risks, otherwise you're bullshit. Bullshit. A succinct and accurate summary. Bravo, Liam. She had called her verbal reticence a rational fear, defined it as a reasonable precaution. It had been exposed as cowardice, as stinginess of heart. She had become a liar by omission; and she couldn't abide liars.

At the echo of footsteps, she stepped up her pace.

She had no car, the trains had stopped running, there were probably no planes to Cork this late. Crying herself to sleep sounded like a hedonistic, satisfying physical release, but if Kevin loved her, she should hurry up and get home before he had time to change his mind.

Stealing a look over her shoulder, she saw the figure was moving rapidly, that it was male. She wondered how long he'd been there.

Her gut tightened. Because she had a superstition concerning resolves. They should be acted on immediately, before the gods could know of your plans and have their last laugh, before fate got the chance to fuck you up. How many times had fate betrayed her in the past, in even so elementary a thing as family? There death had tagged her like a shadow, near but never quite catching up to her. Three years of diligent activity had produced in her no child. It was the idea of precedent, the triumph of experience over hope.

Again, she glanced backward. The man was outside the circumference of direct light. She could tell only that he was of average height, that he moved determinedly and was catching up fast.

She thought of Mick, the trembling of his face, the intensity of his anger, the sudden smell of evil present in so ordinary a man. Jesus.

This trip had been conceived in panic, presided over by an evil genie; that it might end in the ultimate bad luck felt so logical that Katharine couldn't help herself.

She ran.

All these brick fronts were alike, the numbers by the door next to the light: 130, 132, 134, 136. Was the number of her place 138? She couldn't remember. There was no light on 138. Or 140. Or 142. She heard the leaves of a tree rattle, heard the heavy slap of damp shoe on wet sidewalk. At 144 a rosebush reached through the fence and snagged her wool tights. One rough yank left her free, with a gaping view of her bare leg. Number 146 was dark. Number 148. The gate latch stuck, and Katharine vaulted over the picket fence, slipped flat on her ass in the grass, scrambled up, jumped the steps, and leaned into the bell. The door opened immediately and she fell in.

"Are you all right, missus—"

The light from the hall illuminated the man as he passed by, moving with the buoyancy of a happy teenager. He jumped up and slapped the branch of a tree, turned his head their way, and grinned. He *was* a happy teenager. He started whistling in the dark. *Idiot*.

"I'm fine." She looked at Barry. "Peachy keen," she finished dryily, and hoped he'd blame the dampness of her face on the weather. God only knew what he'd make of her ass and stockings.

Too polite to argue, he said, "Ah, well, yes. Perhaps you'd step this way then?" He picked up a tray of chocolates from the hall table, where he'd set them in order to open the door.

Too upset to trust herself questioning him, she followed. In the seconds before he opened the parlor door, she could hear voices, one very loud, one low and deep, one feminine. They were laughing. Barry opened both the double doors. The fireplace was the first thing she saw. It was lit, there were candles and electric light, and it all danced off crystal in a delightful way: bouncing colors and sparkling so that Katharine thought of Mecca in the Fugard play. Dazzled, she caught her breath.

Dierdre said, "You look half-dead. Barry, she must have a cup of tea, wouldn't you say! And look at your shoes! Look at your tights! Out of them right away before you catch pneumonia.''

The old man seated on the chesterfield boomed, "Tea? The gel needs whiskey, can't you see? A good stiff Paddy!''

"Tea and whiskey. There's the only words the grandfather hears with consistency,'' Barry remarked with a lift of his eyebrows.

"He's a man with his priorities straight. We should all be so lucky,'' Bryce said. He'd been sitting on the edge of the chesterfield right in front of her. He stood and put his hands in his pockets.

She was wrong. He wasn't handsome. Not at all. He was beautiful. She threw her arms around him and squeezed so fast, so hard, he lost his balance and they fell back into the brown velvet.

"Ah, yes. He was wondering if you'd be pleased to see him,'' Barry said softly.

"Whiskey!'' the old man shouted. "Whiskey, Dierdre. We all need a jot right about now.''

Fifteen

"Better sit down before you fall down, lad."

Mick jerked his arm away, straightened the suit coat on his shoulders, then went back to his whiskey, refusing to further acknowledge Tommy's steadying hand. Tommy shrugged. Not that he expected thanks anyway, especially from the dour-faced old fart. God, thought he was something, didn't he? Did he think he was threatening him with that crack about the little bit on the side? Jesus. Well, lad, thought Tommy, you shouldn't get too cheeky with me. He knew why Mick had to come clear to Ballsbridge for his drinks; knew the suspicions concerning that nice cushion of funds Mick seemed to have, for a man on disability. And that was another thing! He'd heard Mick say more than once the trouble was his back. He'd had a heart attack! Who did the old fool think he was fooling? No, Mick my boy, a pretty girl might get by with being cheeky in the proper circumstances, but not you. Though it hadn't done Mick any good, had it? The bird wasn't up for the game. Tommy took satisfaction from this, and with the generosity of the successful man to the unsuccessful one who is never likely to be anything else, he let Mick sit in peace while he moved on. It being closing time, he was obliged to encourage folks to leave, much as it pained him.

Putting the glass to his lips, Mick took it away, not having partaken of any of the comfort it had to offer. He stared stonily ahead of him. The roaring in his ears had not completely subsided, and he had been more than a little surprised to find that he'd stayed standing beside his barstool and not raced through a cheering crowd to put that American bitch in her place. Thought she was something, didn't she? He clutched at the scarf folded neatly in its bag next to his whiskey. Suddenly he said, "If you love someone, you want to be with them!"— so loudly he startled Carmel, who was stacking dirty glasses in the sink. "One man for every woman and a woman for every man!" He stopped and fixed on her a penetrating glare. "And what do you think? D'you believe that's true?"

"Ah, sure. That's the way it was intended, wasn't it?"

His eyes were mistrustful, but he gave her a grudging nod of approval. He leaned forward confidentially and proceeded to lecture on his usual topics—the unfairness of the divorce laws, the disintegrating relations between men and women, the morals of the young—while Carmel did the washing up. There was a peculiar sharpness to his lectures, as if in presenting the harshest analysis, he was testing how true her spirit of agreement.

For once, it was nearly true. Carmel's own experience with one of the lads at the far table that evening had left her feeling peevish. The irritation was sure to be temporary, just as the young fellow involved was likely to come around and grant Carmel her due consideration, take more care which way his eyes roamed—at any rate, when Carmel was in the vicinity. In the meantime, Carmel was prepared to listen, since her chores didn't allow her to escape anyway, and go so far as to give a heartfelt sign of accord, now and then.

"Poor old bugger."

"Damned old hypocrite," Tommy countered.

"Sure, that could be true too," Carmel agreed wearily. Her feet hurt. The pub had almost emptied. She and Tommy stood near the entrance to the storage room next to a collection of coats hung on pegs.

"O' course 'tis. Look at him sitting there all sour

grapes because he couldn't put the make on that American."

Carmel bristled like a dog whose territory had been invaded.

"Well, it's no wonder. Takes him for drinks and just struts out of here when she's had her fill. All he wanted was a bit of conversation."

Tommy laughed harshly. "Wanted a bit of something, all right. Wouldn't bet on it being conversation. And what happened to our avid feminist, eh? Looks a bit nasty if you ask me."

"She gives us all a bad name, taking advantage like that," she retorted heatedly.

Enjoying the role of devil's advocate, Tommy said, "Lost her wallet. In an awkward fix."

Carmel snorted.

"And if he's willing to pay, *wanting* to pay—" Tommy shrugged.

"It doesn't matter. She shouldn't have been so stupid. She should have had more dignity than to play up to poor Mick like that."

"And since when did you take such a fancy to Mick?"

"I'm not . . . oh, never mind."

Again, Tommy laughed. "Sounds like old Mick isn't the only sour grapes around here. What's the matter, Carmel dear? Did you lose the attention of one of the lads you've had your eye on, eh?"

She reddened and sputtered, and Tommy laughed harder. She flounced away from him, but Tommy caught her and put his arm around her shoulders.

"He's an irritating old bore and you know it, love. She had her fill and took off—who can blame her? How many times would you have liked to take off in the middle of his bullshit? Come to think of it, you usually do!"

"That's not the point!"

He squeezed her shoulder, but his eye was on the new barmaid, who was bending over a far table, gathering glasses. Carmel caught the look and told him, "You're disgusting, Tommy. A disgrace."

He took his arm away, saying, "And you're the one

to be talking. Just for one night you weren't the center o' the pub's attention, and see what happens to your disposition.''

''Well, fine then,'' she said, and took her coat off a peg. ''I'm going home. I can see you'll be wanting to make sure the new girl's a good worker. Well, let's see how she does with no one but you to instruct her. Break her in properly, will you, Tommy? I suppose that's what you had in mind all along.''

It was. But Tommy was irritated that Carmel should take it upon herself to leave them alone. She was leaving them a lot of clearing up to do. He said, ''Well, if you're going, take your friend with you. The pub's closed, you know. Don't want the garda pounding on my door.''

Just for spite, Carmel stopped and tugged on Mick's sleeve.

''Come on, Mick. Time we got out of here.''

For a moment, as they were stepping out the door, Tommy had half a mind to call them back. He was more sensitive to the moods of his clientele than most would credit. He had to be, for the sake of the pub and good custom. He'd seen a queer look in Mick's eye tonight, especially after Liam and the woman had left. It was a look he'd seen before in men, a kind of warning. He wondered if it was wise to let Carmel walk him even as far as the bus stop. Tommy took a few steps across the pub but then thought, *Fuck it! He wasn't her da, was he?* Serve her right if Mick got funny with her, teach her a lesson. Besides, he had work to do. And afterwards, yes, a drink was in order—to show the new girl he wasn't so hard-hearted as Carmel probably said he was.

He hitched up his pants and went to work.

Sure, Mick had seen Tommy putting his arm around Carmel. And he'd heard the remark about breaking the new girl in properly. Tommy probably broke in all the new girls; even Carmel in her time. Sure. Mick hadn't considered this before, but now that he did, it made sense. It was there for everyone, wasn't it? Except himself. But Mick wasn't going to hold that against her. No. She was a sensitive girl (her joke about stable muck notwithstanding), a good listener. He stayed close to her, making sure the sleeves of their coats touched as they walked, and every so often, rested his hand lightly on the small of her back to guide her through the city streets.

In this quiet neighborhood she needed no guidance, having her bed-sit on one of the side streets near the Berkeley Court Hotel for some time now. There was little of the rowdiness of downtown Dublin after pub-closing time here. A loud voice somewhere in the distance. A drunken girl singing a popular song and doing a cross between a jig and the watusi before a bus on Landsdown Road; stepping in front of it, urging it on while the bus driver hollered and the conductor tried to coax her onto the sidewalk. That was all.

"Wasn't that where you take the bus, Mick?"

"Does a man good to walk. Especially if he's unhappy."

He lifted his chin. He felt if she could only understand how very unhappy he was, she might show him some further kindness—she had invited him to accompany her out of the pub, hadn't she?—they might establish some link. She wouldn't court his company just to let him down. Staring ahead to the dimmer end of the street, contemplating the tragedy of his life, he missed seeing her roll her eyes. She regretted having been aggravated into this. "D'ya understand loneliness, Carmel? What it means to have a point of importance in your life?"

Mick was aware of her sigh and took it as a corresponding gesture of her heart. Such was the power of his wishful thinking and so lost was he in his own need to explain that he talked even of the loss of his job, the blow it had been to be put on disability—"when there was still so much life in him yet," as he was quick to assure her. He was going on about Maire, too, in a pattern so familiar, Carmel could have recited the tale herself and perhaps done a better job of it since Mick had drunk a lot of whiskey and was beginning to ramble. He brought the scarf out of the bag again.

"Ah, Mick . . ." she said.

He'd tagged along with her to the last corner before her destination. The dark brick houses had high hedges along their boundries. Their trees were well established, older than Carmel, or even Mick, for that matter, and not yet completely nuded by fall. The rain had stopped, but left piles of leaves too wet to be stirred by the night breeze. Mick was showing no inclination to leave her to walk the last half block home alone and in peace. The scarf's formerly tidy folds were a muddle in his fingers.

"Carmel, I've been thinking...you'd look lovely..." He draped the scarf artlessly around her neck. The Brown Thomas bag fell from his hand. Powered by the breeze, it skipped lightly up the street.

"Mick, I can't take this," she said, tugging it down the front of her coat. "Look, wrap it up tomorrow and send it to Maire. She'll be pleased—"

Anger distilled alcohol into energy.

"NO! She's lost her chance!"

"You don't mean that, Mick."

"The hell I don't! You don't know. I'll not be made of fool of any longer—"

"Ah, for God's sake, Maire's a good and honest woman; she's not trying to make a fool of you. I don't know what you're expecting her to do—fly all the way from Saudi Arabia for a bloody scarf? One she doesn't know you've bought? Be sensible, will you?" She forced the gift into his shaking hands. "Go home and sleep it off."

She turned to leave him. Tired, she eased up the street, anticipating nothing more exciting than a cup of chocolate, a boiled egg, and bed once she dragged herself home. Mick's steps were quick and unexpectedly light. He had the scarf around her neck and had snapped back her head before she could protest, for he had chosen a long scarf and his reach was good. She clawed at the material, but he had purchased the fabric wisely; wool and silk is very tough. She scratched his face and it had a pleasant sting. He pulled her, kicking, through a break in the hedge, less to hide the activity from the street than to give them a soft place to lie. On a mattress of grass and damp leaves, he pushed her down onto her stomach. He laced the scarf between his fingers and so was able to hold her struggling hands beneath his own. Then he spread his arms so the noose grew very tight and they were in such a position as to make angels in the snow, had there been any. She was jerking and shimmying and trying to twist, and he successfully rode each hump in her movement. It wasn't until then he realized how small she was. She seemed such a presence behind the counter, but she was really such a little bitty thing, he thought, feeling a tide akin to affection as the last spasms of life wrenched her body, as there came the final arch of her back. After she was completely still, he lay there without moving. She was so warm, and he was filled with an amazing sense of resolution, of power. He closed his eyes and breathed in deeply. Then the smell hit him.

He was disgusted to discover she'd shit in her knickers.

Sixteen

"...*I wanted you* to get angry and scream—not necessarily in the Tavern, although I have to admit that was a nice passionate touch." Bryce resumed the ritual of the morning shave. He had a towel wrapped around his waist. Katharine sat on the toilet lid, dressed in a bathrobe. Her chin was resting on her arm, her arm was resting on the edge of the marble vanity. She was watching him shave.

He scrutinized her reflection in the mirror. Hair wet and face makeupless, she was pale. She was also alarmingly thinner. He knew how quickly sick children lost weight but he didn't know it was possible for an adult to lose so much in so few days. When he'd taken her upstairs the night before he hadn't known whether to screw her or feed her. (Common sense had prevailed. It had been too late to go out for a meal.)

Katharine slid off the toilet and crawled over the wet tiles and towels on her hands and knees.

"A wife couldn't be more submissive, more putty in your hands than I am." Her teeth tugged the hem of his towel.

"You are so *full of shit*!" he said, exasperated and losing the towel. Katharine laughed. God, she was all piss and vinegar this morning. Bryce held the razor under the flow of hot water. "Do you want to get married?"

She rocked back on her heels. "No!"

The expression on her face was hardly flattering. Bryce was able to laugh, as though, like a doctor with a hammer at her knee, he'd only been testing her responses. She got up sheepishly and went into the bedroom. She returned and set the ostrich watercolor against the mirror.

"For you," she said.

His hand paused midstroke.

"It's very unusual," he said, eventually. Katharine ducked into the bedroom, presumably to dress. Bryce took the time to rinse the razor and deposit it safely out of convenient reach. "Katharine, when did you buy this?"

"Yesterday, I think," she called to him.

"You went shopping?"

His voice carried quite clearly; hers was muffled.

"Not exactly."

"Not exactly? But you went into a shop to buy this, didn't you?"

"Yes."

"And it wasn't the first shop you went into, correct?"

"Is it correct? Yes, it's correct, all right." Wearing a black turtleneck and zipping a pair of jeans, she appeared at the door.

Bryce pressed the heels of his hands against the marble. He was getting an ulcer and she was browsing the shops, for Chrissake; seeing the sights until he was insane enough to chase after her. He felt foolish standing there stark naked, his face half-covered with foam. And if she put her arms around him, he'd be goddamned before he fell for it this time.

Katharine stayed where she was. "What's wrong?" she asked.

"What's wrong is that when it comes to you, I think with my prick." The bitterness surprised even him. He reached to the floor for a towel.

"Good."

His head snapped up. "Believe me, this is no time—"

"I said, good, I mean good."

She should have had the subtle advantage, having her clothes on. He knew she could look at him and see how vulnerable he felt, know exactly how he was reasoning.

But she was floundering. She opened her mouth to speak and shut it, not accomplishing that end. Finally she shrugged in the direction of the ostrich and said, "I bought this because it looks as foolish as I feel."

Bryce didn't care for the symbolism.

"You bought flowers. What's the difference?"

"The difference is, I didn't buy them. They were ordered by James. I don't need any fucking props. Can you just say you love me and mean it?"

She nodded. He waited.

"Well?"

She hung her head.

"This doesn't exactly seem like the proper circumstances."

"What, *exactly*, constitutes proper circumstances?"

For a half second he tried to tell himself he was only trying to get to the truth. But the truth was, he was being hard on her, he was humiliating her, and he was enjoying it.

"I'm no good at this," she whispered.

"No. You probably never will be. So sometimes you're going to take off and sometimes I'm going to be mean." Ashamed, he pulled her close. "I love you."

She drew back and looked at him. He felt his face grow tight.

"It's not as if you've never heard that before," he told her, defensively.

"But this is the first time cold sober and out of bed." One raised eyebrow announced her sharpened perceptions. "Did you really believe I hadn't noticed?"

He was saved by a knock on the bedroom door. Katharine left him, the expression on her face edged very close to a smirk. She threw a pair of his pants and a shirt into the bathroom. They were followed by a big yellow lily.

Dierdre was at the door.

"Will you be wanting a hot breakfast this morning?" she asked.

She was staring at the top of Katharine's head. Katharine ran her hand through her hair and it came out shaving-cream-coated. She grabbed a towel off the bed.

"Aren't you supposed to be in school by this time?"

"Ah, to be sure, I am. But there was a *murder* just the other side of Landsdown Road, and the grandfather said I should stay home from school today," she said, happy as if the government had declared a national holiday. She was bursting with details. "Strangled, she was. One of my brothers knew her. A fine-looking girl, he said. Worked at one of the pubs down the road. That's when she was killed, coming home from the pub last night, not a block away from her own home. I think that's what upset the grandfather so much, you know. So close and not making it home. The grandfather has very little faith in the garda."

"The garda doesn't know who did it?"

"Sure they do—or so they say. He had to drop dead for them to catch him. Wandered right across the front of the Berkeley Court Hotel—I never noticed, but they have cameras there watching all the comings and goings—and had a heart attack. All roughed up, he was, so they sent someone out to investigate and they found her in the front yard of a house across the street, under a tree. He'd been showing off a scarf in the pub earlier, and that's what she was strangled with. It was still around her neck when they found her. A dead man gives a very brief defense, said the grandfather. He thinks it's all too convenient, the murderer dropping dead before a camera like that. Why should a murderer do the garda such favors?"

"She was murdered with the scarf?" Katharine asked.

"That's what the grandfather was told. One of my brother's friends, Eamon, has just been made inspector, and he stops by whenever he's in the neighborhood for a cup of tea. It's his opinion she was flirting, being no better than she ought to be, and got the man upset when he discovered she was only teasing. The grandfather told him most of us are no better than we have to be, and if that was the penalty for teasing, we'd all be dead except for people lacking a proper sense of humor. Got lively in the kitchen this morning. It's a wonder you didn't hear it.''

"It was rather lively up here this morning," Katharine said dryly. Dierdre looked as if she would have been delighted to be informed on that score, but Katharine went on to say, "Is that new inspector working on the case?"

"Eamon? I don't think Eamon works even when he standing on the very site of the crime. But he's making a good show of it this time. He just finished questioning Tommy down at the pub."

Bryce came out of the bathroom, wiping his face with a towel.

"The murderer was a regular at the pub. Eamon said you'd never think him a murderer. He was such an ordinary man, didn't look as if he'd have the balls for it—those were his words," Dierdre said quickly. "Peevish as an old woman, he told the grandfather. That's what Tommy was after telling him.''

How many pubs were there down the road? There? Four? And how many attended by pretty barmaids? Probably all of them. How many owned by a Tommy? Hard to say. And how many with disappointed men, stubborn and insecure in their opinions, full of drink and resentment? Christ, you could find that anywhere, that wasn't solely Ireland's province. But how many of those disgruntled men had been showing off scarves the night before? Only one.

Suddenly unsteady on her feet, Katharine reached for the footstool, and when she found it, couldn't seem to align her ass to the seat until Bryce and Dierdre lent her a hand.

"Kat, are you all right?"

"She doesn't eat properly," Dierdre said and looked at Bryce as if it was his responsibility to see she did, and as if she perceived that he had failed miserably in his duty.

"I don't think—"

"No, that's all I need. Just some breakfast. Why don't you go ahead and start making it, Dierdre—bacon, eggs, sausage, toast, cereal, brown bread—the lot. I *am* hungry. We'll be down in a minute." She put her head between her knees. Ever practical, Dierdre fetched her a glass of water from the bathroom before she ran downstairs to do as requested.

Bryce watched as Katharine consumed the water greedily. She handed him the empty glass.

"What's wrong?"

She took his head in her hands and talked to him, nose to nose.

"I want to eat a huge breakfast. I want to go to a park, go to a museum, go to the theater tonight, then eat a very good meal in a very good restaurant. I want—"

"Are you going to tell me what this is all about?"

"If you're patient, I'll tell you everything."

He said, "That's all I'm asking."